In her left hand, Rosemary carried the test stick, moving so cautiously it appeared she was afraid the slightest jostle might tamper with the results.

As she approached, Dean offered a supportive nod.

He wished he had the right to take her in his arms as he had that night. In the meantime, he read the stick she handed him. His breath caught and held.

Instantly, his world calmed as he read the results. The thundering hooves slowed and then grew still in his chest. Every tense muscle released. For the first time in a damned long while, he knew exactly what he wanted, and it was exactly what he was getting.

One thin pink line.

Congratulations, Dean Kingsley. You're going to be a father.

Dear Reader,

For a very sweet while, I lived in a kind of latter-day Mayberry, a small town in Oregon still so innocent that the mayor's giant squash provided the lead story on the local news.

Twice a day in the summer, horses pulling a carriage clopped down our block, and in December the locals, dressed in elaborate Victorian costumes, handed out hot cider and chestnuts on the street corner.

Marrying my true love dictated a move—today I make my Mayberry in the middle of a busy city. But I go to work every day in Honeyford, a replica of the wonderful town I lived in.

In *Something Unexpected,* Rosemary is running from her life in the city. Smarting from the pain of lost dreams and broken trust, all she wants is peace. Then she meets Dean Kingsley, Honeyford's favorite son, a man who has played by the rules all his life, but who realizes he may have to bend them a bit to show Rosemary that her home is in his arms.

Welcome to book two of Home Sweet Honeyford!

Wendy Warren

SOMETHING UNEXPECTED

WENDY WARREN

SPECIAL EDITION

Published by Silhouette Books

America's Publisher of Contemporary Romance

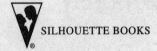 SILHOUETTE BOOKS

ISBN-13: 978-0-373-65587-8

Recycling programs
for this product may
not exist in your area.

SOMETHING UNEXPECTED

Books by Wendy Warren

WENDY WARREN

lives in the Pacific Northwest with her actor husband, their wonderful daughter and the assorted four-legged and finned creatures they bring home.

A two-time recipient of Romance Writers of America's RITA® Award, Wendy loves to read and write the kind of books that remind her of the old movies she grew up watching with her mom and now shares with her own daughter—stories about decent people looking for the love that can make an ordinary life extraordinary. When not writing, she likes to take long walks under leafy trees, lift weights that make her sweat and her husband laugh, settle in for cozy chats with great friends, and pretend she will someday win a million dollars in a bake-off. Check out her website for more information on Honeyford, some great recipes from the townsfolk and other fun stuff. www.authorwendywarren.com.

For Tim, my "something unexpected"
of—oh, lord, is this possible?—twenty-five years.
Despite the fact that I was only five (okay, ten)
when we met, I was fortunate enough to find a man
with sterling qualities I never even thought to look for.
Your integrity, tolerance, compassion
and broad, broad shoulders have never let me down.
My "Mayberry" is in your arms.
I love you.

Chapter One

The Tavern on the Highway
Ten miles west of Honeyford, Oregon
December

"He's a firefighter."

"No way. Ballroom-dance instructor. Specializes in Argentine tango."

"Please. His pants aren't tight enough. And he lacks that chronic self-involved air. He has nice hands. I bet he's a surgeon."

Rosemary Jeffers smiled over the rim of her lemon-drop martini as her three best friends dished about a man at the bar to her right. She didn't turn to look.

The bar scene was not her thing. Neither were lemon-drop martinis, come to think of it, but Ginger Kane, Vi Harris and Daphne Nordli had driven three hours from Portland, Oregon, to Honeyford, intent on rescuing her from a thirty-second birthday that had looked as if it might require the use of antidepressants.

Single, recently relocated and waiting for her new job to begin the following week, she had planned to spend her birthday alone at home, dying the three gray hairs she'd found earlier in the day back to brown.

"Where are we going to eat?" she ventured, attempting for the second time that night to steer the conversation around to her growling stomach.

Vi's red brows swooped in frank disgust. "We're not here to feed our stomachs. We're here to indulge our senses. And yours have been sadly neglected, my friend."

Rosemary shrugged. She did not want to have this conversation. Again. "Taste is a sense. I hear there's a great Italian place—"

"Stop!" Vi slapped her hand on the myrtle-wood table. "We did not doll you up and take you out so you could dribble marinara down your dress. You haven't gone on a date in *two years*. Now turn and look at the dude by the bar. He's been ogling you since we got here."

Daphne nodded eagerly. "He really is a cutie." Two reassuring dimples appeared in her ivory cheeks.

"It *is* time to get back in the dating pool," Ginger added, though she had the grace to look a smidge apologetic.

Rosemary's empty stomach threatened to dry heave. The thought of diving into the dating pool was roughly as appealing as dunking herself in chum and plunging into shark-infested waters.

"I've given dating some thought," she ventured, taking a pretzel from a bowl in the center of the table and sucking salt as she tried to sound offhand. "I've decided not to do it until I find a completely honest man."

She was met with three pairs of wide eyes and a pregnant

pause until Ginger said quietly, "That's going to severely limit your prospects, sweetie."

Rosemary lowered the pretzel to her cocktail napkin while the others reached morosely for their drinks. Of the four of them, only she had married, proving that she'd never *intended* to spend her thirties like a nun. But neither had she planned to return home from work early one evening to find her husband *in flagrante delicto* with his paralegal. That miserable night had occurred two years ago on this very date, which unfortunately had also been her tenth wedding anniversary.

Faith Hill came on the jukebox, singing about the perfect kiss while the aroma of mini tacos wafted from the happy-hour buffet.

"You know what the trouble is?" she pondered aloud, plucking the lemon twist from her martini and winding it until it broke. "The trouble with romance and infatuation and falling in love?" Vi arched a brow. Ginger and Daphne shook their heads. "It isn't that people break your heart because they lie or they leave. What makes you absolutely miserable is the hope that next time will be different. That the next guy is going to be *the* guy, or that 'tonight' is going to turn into 'forever.' Hope," she said earnestly. "That's our problem."

"Wow. That's cynical." Vi tapped a toothpick-speared pearl onion on the edge of her Gibson glass. "I like it. Keep talking."

Rosemary's caramel eyes narrowed. In her chest there was a deep well where her heart used to be, and for too long that well had been filled with confusion and grief. She wanted her heart back.

"I know I don't want to get married again." She tested the words aloud for the first time. "Or even to live with anyone."

"Never?" Daphne looked appalled.

"No." Rosemary shook her head. "Not ever." She felt stronger merely from saying it. "But you're all right about one thing—I shouldn't live like a nun."

"Damn straight," Vi toasted.

"I just have to find a way to date without pain. Like men do."

Disappointed, Ginger reached for her margarita. "I thought you were going to say something profound." She sucked frosty liquid from two skinny red straws, swallowed and proclaimed, "It's not possible to date like men do. Men are born without a conscience. That's why they need women. We're like software—we download guilt onto their brain computers."

Vi stared. "That is seriously twisted." She smiled hugely. "I like that, too." She waved a hand at Rosemary. "You're talking about dating without strings. Been there. In fact, I live there."

"No." Rosemary shook her head. "More than that. I'm talking about dating without hope. No texting girlfriends from the restaurant to see if they'll be your bridesmaids. No doodling potential wedding dates on every scrap paper in sight."

Daphne's hand snaked out guiltily to crumple her cocktail napkin.

"Carpe diem dating," Rosemary improvised like the pitchman of an ad campaign. "When the date itself becomes not simply the means to an end—" she stabbed her finger on the table, punctuating her words "—but the only goal you'll ever have!"

Dead silence followed her big finish. Then Vi stood up and applauded. Ginger followed, albeit more slowly, and Daphne had to be lifted up by the arm. Once they were all standing, Rosemary took a humble bow, and Vi praised, "Brilliant. Show us how it's done."

Resuming her seat, Rosemary laughed. "Maybe I will."

"Not 'maybe.' Right now. The cute dude at the bar hasn't been able to take his eyes off you. He stared the whole time you were talking. I think he just sent over a drink."

The cocktail waitress arrived at that moment with not one, but four peachy-gold drinks she called Honey Slides. The girls approved.

"Very generous," Daphne whispered.

"Good manners." Ginger nodded in approval.

"Wow, that is one sickeningly sweet drink," Vi said after taking the first sip, but she raised the golden concoction and aimed a beautiful smile toward the bar. Before the others knew what she was going to do, Vi crooked one talon-tipped finger and beckoned the man over.

"Vi, no!" Rosemary warned. "We don't even know him."

"Which makes him perfect for your experiment." Abandoning the Honey Slide, she returned to her Gibson. "I dare you to dance with that gorgeous hunk and not allow yourself to think beyond this one night. If you can do that, I promise not to bug you ever again about dating, because clearly you will have proved yourself a more evolved woman than I."

Rosemary looked at her friends' enthusiastic expressions. "You won't bug me *ever* again? Any of you?" They shook their heads. "And then we can go to the Italian place?" Nods all around.

Rosemary knew she wasn't like other women her age, the ones who could flirt, get up and salsa, even touch and kiss men they'd just met. She'd never developed the ability to be casual with males. Spending time, even a little time, with a strange guy in a bar not only would not fill her with hope, it was unlikely to do more than give her a few hives. This was a bet she could win in a walk.

One dance, and they can never pressure me to date again.

She gave it another few seconds of consideration then said quickly, before she could change her mind, "All right. I'll do it."

She was the most stunning creature he had ever seen.

With his back to the bar, Dean Kingsley observed the four vivacious females who shared a table in the sawdust-strewn lounge of Tavern on the Highway. The lady who had caught his interest was not the sexiest of the quartet (that honor belonged indisputably to the redhead), nor did she have the most perfect features (the petite blonde looked like a china doll come to life). But the girl with the dark chocolate curls and the light-as-milk skin was the one he couldn't stop watching.

He'd been studying her for the past half hour, and it had been the most satisfying thirty minutes he'd spent in months.

So far, he'd seen her only in profile, but already he was familiar with several of her mannerisms. She ducked her chin and smiled with her lips closed shortly before she said something that made the other women laugh....

She bit her thumbnail when she was thinking hard then scowled and shook her hand once she realized what she was doing, as if nail biting was a long-standing habit she wanted to break....

She listened carefully when her friends spoke, and she cared about what they were saying....

And, she liked only the salt on pretzels, as the growing stack of soggy sticks on her cocktail napkin attested. That particular habit would wreak havoc on his stash of Rold Gold, but no relationship should be *too* perfect.

Dean grinned. For the first time in weeks, he felt something other than dull resignation. Interest and desire kindled in his body, making him feel alive again. He liked it.

"Forget about her." Len Perris tapped him on the forearm. "She hasn't looked at you once." Tilting his tan Stetson back on his head, Len narrowed his eyes in a thoughtful assessment and nodded. "Go for the blonde. She's an angel. So to speak."

"Which is exactly why he shouldn't go for the blonde." Fred Werblow, Dean's pal from the time he, Len and Fred were all more interested in their rock collections than in women, slapped him on the back. "The last thing our boy needs is an angel. Right, Deano? If you're going to make it through the next two years without wanting to do yourself in then you need a woman who can whip up some excitement." Leaning close, he advised, "Go for the redhead. She looks like a wildcat. Grrrrrr."

"Did you just growl?" Shaking his head, Dean set his draft beer on the bar behind them. The tension he'd momentarily been able to dispel slammed into him again, full force.

"Listen, I don't want to talk about my 'plans' tonight," he said. "I particularly don't want to discuss how or whether I'm going to make it through the next two years." Talking about his predicament, even casually, made his blood pressure spike.

Len put an arm around Dean's shoulders. "That's why we're here, buddy. We're riding shotgun for you."

Fred slapped him on the back again. "That's right. You're being forced to take a wife, and we're going to help you find one you can stomach."

Swearing beneath his breath, Dean hung his head.

His father, Dr. Victor Kingsley, may he rest in peace, had died this past April, leaving a will that bequeathed his sons exactly what they wanted—as long as they married within twelve months of their father's death and remained wed for at least two years.

Afraid his sons might permanently shun marriage, the doctor had prescribed a couple of daughters-in-law.

It was now December. Dean had four months left to marry.

Anyone who knew Dean and his younger half brother would have expected Fletcher to flip the birdie to the will, and Dean to be thoughtful, rational and ultimately compliant. And in fact, that was exactly how the men had reacted—at first. Fletcher had flatly refused to consider marriage, but then, shockingly, he had met someone who'd managed to transform him from gruff loner to tender lover. Two weeks ago, he'd gotten married.

Dean, on the other hand…

Feeling the muscles in his neck contract, Dean considered swapping his beer for bourbon, but he'd never had a taste for hard liquor. Or for escaping life's problems.

After the reading of his father's will, he had forced himself to be practical. A marriage of convenience was not, after all, such a far cry from what he had planned for himself all along.

At thirty-five, he had been engaged once, to a woman as logical and reasonable as he. When Amanda's career had required her to move out of state, they'd ended their relationship, wished each other well—meant it—and had been no worse for the wear. Afterward, Dean had wondered why he'd felt only mildly disappointed when she gave him back his ring.

Eventually, he'd come to accept that deep emotions and powerful yearnings tended to escape him where relationships were concerned. There was only one dream for which he was willing to go to the mat. His father had understood that and was capitalizing on Dean's single passion to coerce him into marriage.

"Maybe Dean's looking for something less permanent tonight. A last hoo-rah." Fred's booming voice was jovial and wholly approving. "Is that why we're here? Do you need to party a little before you settle down? Because no one is going to blame you for that."

Dean sighed. "I'm here because you two wouldn't shut up until I came," he muttered.

What did he want? He wished to God he knew.

Some unnameable impulse tugged his focus once more to the brunette. He'd sent over drinks and each woman had already tasted her Honey Slide. Each woman except for the girl with the curly hair.

I want you.

The answer came so swiftly and clearly that he couldn't refute it.

He wanted to know what she was thinking in this very moment. Why her skin glowed as if she was lit from within. Whether she came here often, why she'd ordered a martini when she didn't seem to like them and what she was doing for the next twenty-four hours, because he wanted to spend them with her.

He saw the redhead toast him, offering a dazzling, if artificial, smile. The brunette didn't even turn around. Dean pushed a responding curve to his lips. *You're welcome,* he nodded to the redhead. It was done. Time to go.

He was about to suggest to Len and Fred that they try the new Italian place in Honeyford, when the brunette stirred. Leaning forward, she put a thumb and delicate forefinger on the fine straws in the frosty drink.

Len said something about barbecue, but Dean only half heard. He waited, gazing like a landlocked sailor staring out to sea, engrossed and longing, hoping for some action to release him from the spell.

And then she moved, turning her head before she lifted her gaze to his. Their eyes caught and held. Eyes the color of butterscotch taffy, big and curious, acquired a spark of surprise when she saw him. Her smile, tentative at first, grew progressively wider and more relaxed, turning the elegant portrait of her face into a masterpiece.

Thank you.

She mouthed the words. Or perhaps he simply couldn't hear her from where he stood.

Thank you was not an invitation to join her, but he wanted to ask her, at least, to dance one dance, to talk, to spend just a few moments getting to know each other before they returned to their real lives. The moments of gazing into her eyes enclosed him in a bubble that floated him lightly above the practical, the mundane. Above his ambivalence about his life and the path that awaited him.

He wanted to remain where he was, sharing a long mutual stare, even if it went no further than that.

But she surprised him.

Raising a loose fist, she briefly rested her knuckles against her mouth, then unfurled her index finger, crooked it, and beckoned him over.

Instantly, Dean knew: though Tavern on the Highway was not a place he frequented, and although he believed much more in free will than manifest destiny, he—pragmatic, level-headed Dean Kingsley—knew that for perhaps the first time in his life he was in exactly the right place at exactly the right time.

Chapter Two

"Here you are, Mrs. Bowman. One copy of *What to Expect in the First Year*." Rosemary twinkled at her heavily pregnant customer. "Just in the nick of time, by the looks of it."

Elliana Bowman placed her canvas book bag atop the checkout desk of The Honeyford Public Library and slid the parenting tome carefully inside. "Two more weeks," she told Rosemary, her handsome, bespectacled face as giddy and enchanted as a child's. "I meant to order the book online months ago. Ordinarily I'm highly organized, but ever since I met my husband, I'm very…distractible."

Her high cheeks turned furiously red, and Rosemary smiled. She hadn't known Elliana at all prior to the other woman's marriage to Dan Bowman, Honeyford's resident mechanic, but she'd been told that although Dan and Elliana had lived in Honeyford all their lives, they hadn't hooked up until they were solidly in their thirties. Now they were expecting their first child.

Rosemary waited for the pangs of envy she used to feel when confronted with another woman's pregnancy. Through her teens and her twenties, she'd been certain that motherhood was her mission.

Not anymore. Her mission now was her work, and the residents of this darling town she'd been fortunate enough to find were becoming her makeshift family.

"I'm going to make myself a note," she told Elliana, "to renew that book for you automatically if you don't return it on time. You just enjoy your pregnancy and don't worry about a thing."

Elliana beamed, waving goodbye as she left, and Rosemary told herself once again how lucky she was.

"Plug your nose! Incoming!"

Rosemary turned to see her assistant, Abby, a twentysomething library clerk who wore shoulder pads and had a predilection for World War II novels, approach the circulation desk. In one hand, Abby held a book as far from her body as possible. With the thumb and forefinger of her other hand, she pinched her nostrils shut.

"Brady Silva just upchucked on *Captain Underpants,*" Abby announced nasally. "His mother's in the bathroom, cleaning him up."

"Oh, dear."

Glancing at the grandfather clock that, Rosemary was told, had graced the entrance of the Honeyford Public Library for more than fifty years, she felt a rush of relief when she saw there were only seventeen minutes left to closing time. Since beginning her job as head librarian here, she'd stayed late more nights than not, finding any number of delightful tasks to perform. In two months, she had implemented a new literacy

program benefiting local youth and had several more programs planned. She didn't mind staying late.

Her sole motivation for wanting to leave on time tonight
was the flu that had been snaking through Honeyford like
one of the evil Dementors in Harry Potter. Because she'd felt
funky on and off since morning, Rosemary feared she, too,
might be coming down with the bug. Brady Silva's accident
with the book made her more than a little queasy.

"Not to worry." Rosemary reached for one of the used
plastic shopping bags she kept beneath the desk, shook it open
and had Abby drop the book inside.

"We'll all be puking by tonight." Abby shook her head,
depositing the book and plucking a moistened wipe from the
box Rosemary kept on the counter. "My fiancé has it, too.
The first twenty-four hours are sheer misery."

Rosemary swallowed. She detested throwing up. "Wash
your hands with soap and hot water every hour for as long as
it takes you to sing 'Happy Birthday,' and whatever you do,
don't touch your eyes, nose or mouth."

Abby gaped at her. "Are you phobic or something?"

"Germs can live eleven hours on nonporous surfaces like
door handles, steering wheels and shopping carts. I'm not
phobic—I'm cautious."

Abby's full lips twitched at the corners. "Cautious about
everything or just germs?"

"Every—" Rosemary stopped abruptly.

Almost three months ago, she would have completed that
sentence without a second thought. *I'm cautious about everything.* Now she avoided her clerk's curious gaze and muttered, "It's still cold-and-flu season. It can't hurt to take extra
precautions."

Nodding, Abby moved off to return a stack of books to the
large-print section. Rosemary pressed a computer key so she
could check in DVDs, but her mind was a mile away.

Make that ten miles and two and a half months away.

As if she'd pressed a play button in her brain, her head filled with images.

Tavern on the Highway...Faith Hill on the jukebox...a drink called a Honey Slide that she'd barely touched...and a man named Dean, whom she had touched a lot, in ways she would never, not in a million years, have imagined she could touch a stranger.

Not that he had remained a stranger for long.

By the time the library closed and Rosemary was able to head to her car, she had replayed that night with Dean a dozen times...and felt herself blush almost as many.

That evening in the bar, she had intended to thank the tall, handsome man for the drinks, perhaps to chat just a bit so the girls wouldn't rag on her later and then to say goodbye. That was all. Harmless.

Seated in her car, alone in the library parking lot, Rosemary clapped her hands over her face and groaned.

After dancing, Dean had escorted her back to her table and chatted amiably with her friends, but his demeanor with them had been nothing more than courteous. Brotherly. So different from the way he'd looked at her. They had returned to the dance floor again and again. At some point in the evening, leaving the bar with him had seemed perfectly sane. In her entire adult life, she could not recall feeling the sexual urgency she'd felt that night.

Flushing anew at the memory, Rosemary flipped her visor down to check her face in the mirror. Mascara was smudged beneath her eyes. Licking a finger, she carefully wiped it away and thought that if she lived a hundred more years, she would not understand how she had morphed in one evening from the woman who never went anywhere without her AAA card, cell phone, a calling card in case the cell phone went dead and at least half a dozen quarters in the event the calling card didn't work, to the woman who jumped into the arms and the bed of a total stranger.

Despite her brave talk of carpe diem dating, in her heart the words *casual* and *sex* were antonyms.

Now somewhere in the world there was a man with whom she had gotten naked and made love with the lights on, yet whose last name, age, address and occupation she still did not know.

What kind of woman did that?

"The kind who's finally joined the twenty-first century," Vi had assured her approvingly the day after.

Right. The kind who believed in carpe diem dating. No strings. No hope. And no recriminations.

That last part was gonna take a while.

Lifting her head, Rosemary turned the key in the ignition, gripped the steering wheel with fingers stiff from the March chill and threw the car into Reverse.

Chicken soup.

The sudden craving for something warm, uncomplicated and comforting gave her a direction, and she headed for Sherm's Queen Bee, the grocery store on the east end of town. With a population of nearly nineteen hundred people, Honeyford was large enough to support two markets. Sherm's was the larger, and it stayed open later.

On her way into the store, Rosemary grabbed a handled basket. The act of shopping distracted her from troubling thoughts. By the time she'd picked up aspirin, tea and orange juice, she felt a bit better. Grabbing a box of saltines from the cracker aisle in case her nausea returned, she started toward canned soups, one aisle over, when she overheard a conversation that managed to make her smile.

"You do not need to use canned soup to make macaroni and cheese." The woman's voice was vehement and vaguely disgusted. "Get a good English Cheddar."

"Cheddar-cheese *soup* makes it feel more like comfort food, Amanda," came the man's much gentler reply. "Trust me. This is the best mac and cheese you'll ever taste. You'll feel like you're ten again."

"I don't want to feel ten again...."

Rosemary laughed to herself. Right there was one of the perks of being single. She used to use cheddar soup to make macaroni and cheese, but Neil had loathed that particular meal, saying it tasted "cheap." During the first year of their marriage, she'd found a recipe for fettuccini Alfredo and had abandoned her beloved mac and cheese altogether.

With no need to please anyone but herself tonight, and hungry for the first time all day, she skirted a display of Goldfish crackers and rounded the soup aisle, intent on making a big casserole of creamy pasta tonight. She wanted to thank the gentleman with the macaroni craving for reminding her about this treat and then tell him to grab his own can of soup and run, before he spent the better part of his life acquiescing to someone else's desires, but, of course, it was none of her beeswax.

As she entered the aisle, Rosemary couldn't help but glance at the woman with the firm opinions on cheese and the strongly judgmental tone. Tall enough to partially block Rosemary's view of the man, the blonde wore black-rimmed glasses, a belted coat, stiletto-heeled leather boots and a perturbed expression. "I'm going to call Beezoli's and have them make a fettuccini Alfredo to go," she said as she fished her cell phone from her pocket. "Do you want one?"

Hiding her grin, Rosemary stepped in front of the couple to reach for the soup. "Excuse me."

As she straightened, she angled her body, hoping to take a quick, nosey-bones peek at the man. Good English Cheddar was clearly a gal who got her own way. The poor guy might never enjoy a decent mac and cheese again.

Sorry, buddy, she told him mentally as she turned, deciding to give him a smile. *Believe me, I relate—*

Dear God!

The can of soup dropped from Rosemary's hand, clunking onto the hard floor.

She stared stupidly, frozen as a statue, while Dean Whose-Last-Name-She-Did-Not-Know stared back at her.

"You dropped something," the blonde intoned drily, which should have snapped Rosemary out of her stupor, but didn't.

Dean, however—as neatly groomed and handsome as he'd been two and a half months ago—dived for the can of soup, rose and handed it back to her, his blue gaze glued to her face.

"Hello," he said.

She should have recognized his voice right away. Smooth and rich rather than deep, like the best milk chocolate, it had wrapped her in delicious sensation that magical night.

Rosemary couldn't answer him. Her mind buzzed with a dozen questions.

Do you live in Honeyford?

Does Good English Cheddar live in Honeyford?

Were you and she together when you and I…?

Mortified, by the possibility that she had slept with another woman's man, Rosemary could feel her face flush and perspiration build beneath her heavy clothing.

"Do you two know each other?" The blonde sounded bored as she flipped her hair back and brought her cell phone to her ear.

Rosemary glared at Dean. He seemed not to have heard his companion's question. His brows lowered in deep thought.

She turned toward the woman, wondering whether she should answer, then saw something that strangled any words that might have emerged.

From the hand holding the phone, a simple ring glittered. A simple, emerald-cut diamond engagement ring.

Fury sped through Rosemary's veins like fire along a line of gasoline.

"We should do this again…for the next forty years." The words he'd murmured while they'd danced came back to taunt her.

She knew better than to trust in forever. That was one reason she'd left before dawn—so she wouldn't be tempted to buy into a fairy tale. But she'd assumed, at least, that her prince-for-a-night was as charming and decent as he'd seemed.

Snake! Rat! Philanderer! She was tempted to pick up the can of cheddar-cheese soup and aim it at his head, but then another thought struck. Because of Dean's dishonesty, she had done to another woman what had been done to her. She had become a mistress by mistake!

The blonde—Amanda, was it?—lowered her chin, peering at Rosemary above her rectangular glasses. "Are you all right? You look like you're going to pass out. Dean, take out your phone in case you have to call 9-1-1. Beezoli's has me on hold."

The last thing Rosemary saw before she turned and ran through the store was Dean's hand reaching toward her. As she chucked her basket of goods and raced for the door, she heard him call, "Rosemary, wait!"

And then Amanda's voice, more faintly: "You *do* know her."

For the third morning in a row, Rosemary huddled on her side beneath a fluffy white comforter ninety minutes past the time her alarm went off. She'd missed two days of work, and now, on her regularly scheduled day off, she could no longer deny the facts: from the moment she opened her eyes in the morning, nausea hit so hard she could barely raise her head.

She'd thought she had the flu that was going around, but by midday she typically got better, and around dinnertime she was ravenous…only to begin the cycle again the next day.

And, she'd missed two periods.

At first, she'd chalked the interruption to her monthly cycle up to the stress of her recent move and a new job. Now it seemed far more ominous than that.

Grunting, Rosemary pushed the covers aside and slowly sat up. Her feet had barely touched the hardwood floor when her stomach rebelled, and she raced to the bathroom.

"I hate throwing up," she told her sad reflection as she brushed her teeth after the fact. More than anything, she wanted to crawl back into bed, pull the pillows over her head and stay there.

She'd worked so hard to create a new life for herself after her divorce. Now, if her suspicion proved correct, that sweet new life was going to turn into a very bad soap opera.

"Stupid, stupid, stupid!" Sniffing back tears, she returned to the bedroom to get dressed. She hadn't been on birth control since her divorce. There hadn't been any need since she hadn't intended to be sexually active.

On that now deeply regretted night in December, she and Dean had used a condom….

The first time. And the second.

But the third? She honestly couldn't remember.

A glance in the mirror above her dresser told Rosemary that she looked like death warmed over. She shrugged as she dressed in jeans and a heavy wool sweater then twisted her curly hair into a knot atop her head. From her hall closet, she withdrew a shin-length camel-hair coat with a collar she could turn up to partially hide her face, and a pink cloche that she tugged down around her ears.

Honeyford wasn't small enough to run into people one knew every day, but she hoped to minimize the odds that someone in this quaint, conservative town might stop her to strike up a conversation as she ran her errand: the purchase of an at-home pregnancy test to determine whether she was knocked up from a one-night stand with an engaged stranger.

Grabbing her purse and heading into the brisk March day, Rosemary fought back tears once again. She'd thought her divorce was the low point in her life. Now she was deeply afraid she was about to hit a new bottom.

It took ten minutes to walk from her home on Oak and 4th Street to downtown Honeyford. As a string of bells jingled merrily against the glass door of King's Pharmacy, Rosemary began to wish she'd driven to another town to make her purchase.

It certainly didn't escape her that if Dean and his fiancée lived in Honeyford then she was likely to bump into them again sooner or later. She comforted herself with the knowledge that this was a workday for most people, and given that it had taken her over two months to run into Dean the first time, she could reasonably expect luck to be on her side today.

In fact, if she was *really* fortunate, her nausea would turn out to be some exotic disease or possibly intermittent salmonella or merely garden-variety stress. Anything other than pregnancy. And then she could simply ignore her one-night stand and his bride-to-be the next time she saw them.

Quickly, Rosemary entered the store, which was larger than she'd expected, with an old-fashioned soda fountain to her left and gift shop up front. A cash register was located at the entrance, but also, she saw as she made her way back, in the rear of the store by the pharmacy.

Locating the aisle with the EPTs, Rosemary grabbed two boxes to be on the safe side then gathered a few additional items before she approached the cash register near the pharmacy.

The cashier had teased, bright red hair and pince-nez glasses perched low on the end of her nose. Her forehead creased deeply as she perused an issue of *OK! Magazine.* Rosemary never forgot a face and took a relieved breath when she realized the woman was a stranger to her.

Unloading her items onto the counter, she slid a large box of candy ahead of the EPT. In addition she'd selected a white teddy bear holding a sign that read Friends Forever, and a greeting card, reasoning that if she did see someone she knew, she could say she was on her way to give moral support to a friend whose husband was overseas, and who thought she might be pregnant and didn't want to be alone when she found out.

Hopefully, it would sound better coming out of her mouth than it did in her head.

A forced smile strained her lips as she mumbled her "Hello."

The cashier greeted her without fanfare and efficiently rang up the purchase. "Thirty-two ninety-five."

She hadn't reacted in the slightest to the EPTs. Rosemary relaxed, realizing she'd been paranoid. This was a pharmacy, after all. They probably sold EPTs all the time.

"Thirty-two ninety-five," she repeated with more spring in her voice, opening her purse.

"I don't think I have a bag large enough for the candy box," the older woman muttered, peering beneath the counter. "Do we have any of those gift bags left from Valentine's Day?" she called out.

Opening her deep handbag, Rosemary fished for her wallet.

From the pharmacy behind the cash register, someone responded, "Why don't you head on up to the front now, Millie. I'll look for the bags."

As Rosemary registered the warm male voice, the strangest

feeling she had ever experienced overcame her. Fire ignited in her belly and rushed through her veins so quickly that for a moment she felt as if she might pass out.

No. Please, no.

Impulse almost compelled her to look up, but she resisted, keeping her head as low as possible.

"I don't need the bag," she protested to the cashier even as the woman walked around the counter. "I'll just pay, and—"

"Dean will take care of you, honey."

Dean.

Ohmygod, ohmygod, ohmygod.

As the older woman walked away, Rosemary's gaze zeroed in on the EPT, which seemed to be glowing like a flare. She couldn't breathe.

Frantic, she looked around for a way to hide the evidence. Eye-level to her right were rolls of vitamin C and throat lozenges. *Too small.* Below them hung bags of cough drops.

Diving, she seized several bags, dumping them on the counter. By the time a white lab coat appeared in her field of vision, there was barely an inch of counter surface visible. Tugging her hat as low as it would go, Rosemary dug through her purse. *Where was her damned wallet?*

"All right, how large a gift bag do we need?" Dean inquired pleasantly as he halted in front of her. With only the counter to separate them, Rosemary felt her entire body tense. Her *engaged* lover was the friendly neighborhood pharmacist.

Surveying her goods, he whistled. "Looks as if you're medicating quite a cough." He picked up one of the packages. "These are fine for a cough related to the common cold, but if you're treating the bug that's going around, you'll need something stronger. May I recommend a couple of products I think will be more effective for you?"

Oozing compassion and care, his voice could make a

woman believe she was safe in his hands. An excellent trait in a pharmacist; a treacherous quality in a lover.

"No need," Rosemary croaked, morphing her normal tones into something that resembled a bullfrog on Marlboros. "I'm stocking up."

What were the chances she could pay her bill, collect her items and leave without having to look up?

"Rosie?"

Her trembling fingers closed around the wallet, and she felt a mustard seed's worth of relief. Pulling out several bills, she tossed them onto the counter, opened her wide-mouthed purse and began sweeping her purchases inside. She had no hope that everything would fit, but prayed she could get the EPT in there without Dean noticing.

"I've been looking for you," he said. "Where have you been all these months?"

Her hand froze. "You've been looking for me for *months?*"

"Since December."

Anger raced through her, and she stared at him, hard. As always, Dean's face was incredibly handsome, but this time the attractiveness was blunted by the fact that he was a low-down, lying boy-slut.

All through her divorce, Rosemary had preferred to skirt issues rather than to confront them, afraid her feelings would overpower her. Now she experienced no such compunction.

"I wonder how you had the time to look for me?" she said. "Didn't your *fiancée* have plenty for you to do?"

She gave him points—but only a couple—for not trying to deny the existence of a fiancée. Neil had lied even after she'd caught him red-handed.

He frowned. "I want to explain—"

"Good," she interrupted. "You can start by explaining *me* to *her.*" She reached again for the items on the counter, righteous indignation—no, rage—trumping all other emotion.

Cheating didn't ruin only the immediate relationship: it robbed the cheated-on person of her dreams. If you'd loved and been lied to once, it was damned difficult to trust in love a second time. Rosemary actually felt a kinship with Good English Cheddar.

"Hey, stop." Dean reached for her forearm. "Don't run away again. Talk to me."

She sent him a withering glance. "You have got to be kidding. Let go of my arm."

"Rosemary, is that you?"

Oh, good lord.

Dean let her go, and Rosemary unclenched her gritted teeth to smile limply at the new arrival. Irene Gould, a regular participant at the library's book club approached the pharmacy counter. "Hello, Irene."

"Darling girl! The book club has been so worried about you. We heard you have that awful flu that's going around. Are you better?" she asked.

"Yes," Rosemary lied. "Doing fine."

"Oh, good. Listen, darling, I won't be at the library this Thursday. I'm going on a seniors' bus trip to Portland. We're touring the Chinese Garden and eating dim sum in China Town."

Rosemary nodded politely, acutely aware that Dean was listening to every word. To him, Irene said, "You make sure she goes home with vitamin C and zinc. We want our librarian back."

"I'll make sure," Dean murmured pleasantly enough.

The moment Irene left, Rosemary reached again for the items on the counter. This time Dean grabbed her wrist and held on tight.

"You work at the library? That's where you've been all this time?"

"Let go of my wrist," Rosemary ordered, looking up, but if

Dean heard her, he gave no indication. His attention lowered, riveted now on the goods rather than on her. With his free hand, he extracted from the pile of cough drops and candies one of the two EPT test boxes.

Panic turned Rosemary's body cold. Thoughts ran through her mind so quickly, she couldn't pin one down.

"It's for a friend," she blurted. "A friend who thinks she might be pregnant and doesn't want to be alone when she finds out." The fib she'd prepped in case she ran into anyone she knew rolled off her tongue before she could think twice. "Her husband's out of the country, so I said I'd bring along a pregnancy test...."

"And cough drops?"

"Those are mine. I've been sick."

"Maybe you should see a doctor." He studied her. "But make it an ob-gyn." His expression was somber. "Your nose turns red when you're lying."

Chapter Three

Her ears turned red, too.

A blush infused her cheeks, and her eyes began to glisten.

Dean sensed her genuine panic and confusion; he'd have liked to comfort her, but he had his own teeming emotions to deal with. How many weeks ago had they met? *Ten.* Anything could have happened since that night. Anything could have happened before. He knew so damn little about Rosie or her lifestyle, yet when he looked from the EPT box to her eyes, he was certain she was purchasing the test because of their night together.

Frustration tightened his gut. For weeks he had tried to find her, never realizing she worked less than a mile from the building on Main where he worked and lived.

She'd run out on him after a night filled with passion, had bolted as soon as she'd recognized him in the market and obviously wanted nothing to do with him now. And still when he looked at her he felt something he almost never felt: need. An interest and desire and hope that weren't matched anywhere else in his life.

"Where did you go?" he asked.

"Back to my real life."

When he'd woken to find her side of the bed empty, he'd considered a number of possible scenarios: she was married; she had an appointment she couldn't break; he had been a disappointing lover. Remembering her reactions to him, he felt safe discarding the latter scenario, but if it was true, he wanted another chance.

Frustration made his chest muscles ache when he realized how eager she was to escape the pharmacy. Red splotched her cheeks under her crazy pink hat, and her eyes—which still reminded him of candy—refused to meet his.

Talk to me. I've been looking for you for weeks.

Letting her go, he yanked a bag from beneath the counter and packed most of Rosie's items inside. He slid the EPT into his pocket.

He needed to tell her about Amanda, but they had other business to attend to first.

"Come on."

"What?" She shook her head. "I'm not going anywhere with you."

"Polly!" he called to a young woman stocking a shelf nearby. The girl, a teenager who'd worked for him the past two summers, loped over. "Ask Millie to come back and man the pharmacy for a while while you stay up front. I'm taking a break."

"Sure thing." Polly smiled at him then looked at Rosie. "Oh, hi, Ms. Jeffers! I didn't recognize you in that hat. It's awesome."

Rosie nodded, obviously dismayed at being seen by yet another person. Dean used her discomfort to his advantage.

"Ms. Jeffers and I have some business to take care of. We'll be upstairs if anyone needs us." He stared at her. "Right?" he demanded softly.

Rosie's jaw clenched, but she accurately read his expression: he wasn't going to let this go. If she left, he'd follow, sooner or later. Probably sooner.

"Right." The word barely emerged through her gritted teeth.

Good enough.

"If you'll follow me, Ms. Jeffers." Dean walked around the counter and toward the stairwell leading to his apartment above the pharmacy. At least now he knew her last name and place of employment. And strangely, although he was about to take a pregnancy test with a woman he barely knew, he suddenly felt more optimistic than he had in weeks.

As he walked away, Rosemary sweltered beneath her winter clothing and an even more cumbersome layer of embarrassment. She felt hot, apprehensive and foolish.

"I'm bringing my friend an EPT…and some cough drops…" What a dork! She was an awful liar, which was why she hadn't fibbed since she'd failed to complete a book report in fourth grade and told her teacher it got ruined when her mother washed her backpack.

Dean appeared about as convinced as Mrs. Karp had been. Seeing him again while she was trying to ascertain whether she was pregnant with his child had quite simply sent her into a flight-or-fight panic.

Hesitating before she followed him, Rosemary dug all the cough-drop bags from her purse and returned each one to its peg. The cashier had not rung them up, and while Rosemary might be a woman of questionable judgment, she was no shoplifter. She had allowed her ex-husband's treachery to turn her into someone she was not: a woman who spent the night with a total stranger. Whatever happened now—whatever the pregnancy test revealed—she was going to reclaim her former integrity.

Dean reappeared at her side. "What are you doing?"

"Returning these things. The cashier didn't ring them up, and I don't need them."

"Okay." He watched her a moment then said, "I'll be right back." When Rosemary was placing the last bag of cough drops on its hook, Dean returned, holding a small rectangular box. Another EPT test, but a different brand. "This one is more accurate," he informed her stoically. "So I'm told."

Rosemary eyed the box. "You have experience with this," she concluded darkly.

"Not personally, no. I'm a pharmacist. My customers talk to me."

Rosemary knew she had no right to judge. She was as responsible as he for the fact that she was about to pee on a stick. But at least she wouldn't be *engaged to somebody else* when she got the results.

"I don't have any experience with this, either," she blurted. "This isn't something I've done before."

Dean's brows rose. "No kidding?" He tilted his head toward the cough drops she'd hastily replaced. "You were so smooth purchasing the EPT I never would have guessed."

Rosemary flushed. "I mean, I don't have experience with *needing* to buy one. I don't do…what we did. I don't go to bars, and I don't go home with men. Just for the record."

"I see." His blue eyes, as placid as a summer sky, glowed with gentle humor. "Well, just for the record, I didn't think you did, Rosie."

The night they'd met she had told him to call her Rosie, though no one who knew her well used that nickname. For that single evening, she had wanted to be someone different, someone more frivolous, someone who didn't weigh out each decision as if it would have an effect on national security.

His lips edged into a smile that reminded her of his kisses, which had felt like conversation, as if he'd been speaking to her with each press of lips.

He had held her in the dark of early morning, and after his breath had steadied in her ear, she'd lain awake, bewildered by the fact that the most passion she'd ever experienced had happened in the arms of a stranger.

Frightened by the burgeoning desire to turn their single night into something more meaningful, she'd eased out from beneath his heavy arm and the leg he'd slid over hers. Then she'd gotten dressed and left, attempting to put the evening in perspective: she'd made a mistake. She had slept with a man she did not know, who had picked her up in a bar. Better to chalk it up to experience than to turn it into something it wasn't. So, she had decided to go home, shower and take a vow of chastity.

And that was before she'd seen him with another woman.

Remembering that she was a train wreck when it came to judging a man's character, Rosemary nodded to the EPT in Dean's hand and said, "If you'll give me that, I'll let you know what happens."

"You can take the test here."

Incredulous, she shook her head. "In a public restroom?" Her gaze darting furtively, she lowered her voice. "Are you nuts? I would think that you, even more than I, would want to be as discreet as possible. You're a pharmacist. People have to trust your judgment."

Tall, square-shouldered in his white lab coat and looking impossibly composed under the circumstances, Dean raised a brow. "That's never been a problem. And, no, not in a public restroom. There's a private bathroom upstairs."

"I have a private bathroom at home. I'll call you."

The friendly humor in Dean's eyes dimmed. "We took the risk together—we can find out the result together."

Before she could protest again, he added, "Humor me. If the result is negative, we never have to see each other again. Unless you need a prescription filled."

And if the result is positive?

What was he going to say and how was he going to react if the thin pink line appeared? Rosemary, if she'd had the option, would have preferred to find out over the phone. Or by email.

"It might help to have time to process the information on our own."

He shoved a hand through his hair, ruffling the brown waves. "Look, I'm as out of my element here as you are. Let's get this part done right now. We'll have the rest of the day to 'process.'"

The bells at the front of the store jingled again and happy voices filled the pharmacy. Rosemary didn't want to discover whether they were going to be heading in her and Dean's direction. "All right, all right. Let's go."

She was rewarded with one of the calming smiles that doubtless made every spoonful of medicine he parceled out to his customers go down more easily.

"This way," he said and headed to a staircase that led to the building's second story.

Trepidation made Rosemary's legs feel like lead weights. Her anxiety mounting with each step she took, she followed Dean to a single door at the top of the stairs and stood beside him on the landing as he unlocked the door and pushed it open.

"What is this?" she asked as the open door revealed an attractive living room.

"My apartment."

"You live here?" Being in the pharmacy with him was

bad enough. She did not want to be alone with Dean in his home.

Pocketing the keys again, he winked at her. "I can walk to work. Plus, it's only me, Buff and Calamity up here, and we don't take up a lot of space."

"Buff and Calamity. Buffalo Bill and Calamity Jane?"

Stepping back so she could enter, he smiled more broadly. "Exactly. My fish. I don't have enough space for a dog, and I kill plants, but the fish and I have been together so long they're almost fossils."

Rosemary crossed the threshold of the apartment with all the momentum of sap trying to move *up* a maple tree. The room was attractive, with an exposed brick wall and handsome furniture, but her anxiety turned everything sort of fuzzy.

Three steps in, she turned to him. "Look, I do not belong here. It isn't right." *And why was he so damned composed, anyway?* Seeing no point in quibbling, she hit him with her best shot. "Engaged men should be with their fiancées, not with other women. I can't imagine that your fiancée would be okay with the fact that I'm here, much less—" she lowered her voice and hissed again "—with the reason for it."

Dean plowed fingers through his hair then dragged his hand down his face. He also winced.

Crossing her arms, Rosemary waited. Caught red-handed. She'd give him a minute to try to wriggle out of it then take her test kit and go.

"I'm not engaged, Rosie. I was," he hastened to add before she could respond. "We called it quits two days ago."

She was surprised, but hardly placated. "That's two and a half months too late," she pointed out. "You should have called it quits *before you slept with someone else.* And for the record, it is not fair to 'the other woman' not to *tell* her she's the other woman. Some people believe women should stand together, not destroy each other's lives."

Dean shut his front door. "Wait a minute. You think I was engaged the night I met you?"

"Oh, please." Rosemary shook her head firmly. "Don't put a spin on it. Whether you were engaged then or still dating, you belonged with her, not me. I've heard every rationalization there could possibly be for cheating, and they're all bull. There is no justification for that kind of dishonesty."

"You've been cheated on?"

Rosemary stiffened. Concern turned Dean's features into his the-doctor-is-in expression that had hooked her in December.

"We're talking about *you*," she said.

"Come sit down." He gestured toward a chocolate-colored leather sofa. "I'll try to explain."

"I don't need an explanation. I only wanted you to know how I feel about being drawn into this kind of situation."

"There was no situation when I met you, Rosie." Dean's gaze bore into her as he made sure she understood. "Amanda and I were engaged two years ago. Six months into it, we broke up when her job transferred her to Minnesota. I didn't see her again until a few weeks ago."

Rosemary blinked dumbly as she processed the information. Dean hadn't been engaged to or even dating Good English Cheddar on the night she and he had had their fling? That was excellent news. She wasn't a home wrecker.

And yet…

"You hadn't seen each other for a year and a half, yet you got engaged again in only a few weeks?" She wanted to bite her tongue the moment the words were out, because she understood exactly why she'd asked: she didn't like the idea that he had that passion with someone else. "Never mind. It doesn't matter."

"I wasn't in touch with Amanda in any way when you and I were together." Dean had a disconcertingly direct gaze when he needed to make a point. "Trust is something I take seriously."

Captured by his words and his gaze, she wished he hadn't said that. Without the specter of infidelity, he was once again the strong, attentive stranger who gave more than he took when they made love and who managed to make her feel more comfortable in her own skin than she'd felt in ages.

They stared at each other, lost for words and unsure of their next actions. Then Dean pulled the EPT box from the pocket of his lab coat. Looking down, he turned it over in his hands, and Rosemary knew that one way or another, they had to have an answer. She asked him where his bathroom was.

He extended an arm. "This way."

He seemed to think she was going to precede him to his restroom, but that was where Rosemary drew the line.

Holding out her hand, she gestured to the box. "I'll take that now."

Expecting an argument, she was relieved when all he said was, "Right," and handed the test kit to her.

She progressed slowly down the indicated hallway, feeling more surreal with each step. The only comfort she could dredge up was the knowledge that if she hadn't gotten pregnant in ten years of marriage, it was unlikely Dean had gotten the job done in a single night.

"Rosie."

Nearly jumping when she heard her name, she turned.

He stood with his hands in his pockets, his brows drawn together, even features awash in concern. "Good luck."

For a moment they were comrades, and even though they were bonded by what both now surely viewed as a colossal mistake, Rosemary felt less alone.

She managed a brief smile. "You, too."

Entering the bathroom, she closed the door, sending up a prayer that in just a few minutes all this would be over.

* * *

As Rosemary disappeared from the hallway, the ghost of her frightened smile gave Dean a physical ache.

Immediately after the words *good luck* had left his lips, he'd realized he wasn't sure what kind of luck he was hoping for.

March in eastern Oregon was a cold state of affairs, but Dean began to perspire as if it were August in the Everglades. He wanted to phone someone right now—his sister-in-law, perhaps, or maybe his brother—someone to whom he could confess, *I may have a pregnant woman in my apartment, and I think…that would be okay.*

For weeks he had looked for Rosie, returning to Tavern on the Highway on the off chance he would see her there again. He'd realized the night he met her that she didn't frequent the place, but hoped he might run into one of her friends. He'd grilled every bartender and all the servers about the women, appearing, he was certain, like a stalker, but he hadn't cared. Looking for her—and, when he wasn't looking for her, thinking about her—became his primary occupation. And then Amanda had shown up.

Glancing at his watch, Dean wondered if he ought to offer to time the test for Rosie.

Yeah, she's in there hoping you'll hover.

With restless fingers, he rubbed his temples. Love had never been easy for him—a congenital defect, apparently, which both he and his younger brother had inherited. Fletcher, however, was married now and, as unlikely as it seemed, he had become a devoted father to the three children from his lovely wife's first marriage. Claire Dobbs Kingsley had turned Dean's bad-tempered half brother into the proverbial pussycat. It hadn't been easy, and it had come about only because Fletcher had been forced to wed.

Inexplicably, Fletcher was in a marriage of convenience that had turned into a union of souls.

Consciously exhaling, Dean knew he hadn't breathed properly since the day he'd read his father's will and discovered that Victor Kingsley required each of his two sons to marry or lose what they loved most—in Fletcher's case, the ranch that had been in his mother's family for generations; in Dean's case, the building in which he now stood.

Ironically, Fletcher had been the one who had seethed over the will, refusing at first to abide by its dictates. Dean, on the other hand, had quickly reconciled himself to a marriage of convenience. Why not? He'd never been impetuous, was not prone to infatuation and seriously doubted his capacity to fall head-over-heels in love. He'd been involved in a few longer relationships; no one had ever broken his heart.

He had an excellent career, a good life. He was only deficient when it came to love, but at least he knew it. Therefore, a marriage of minds and shared values, a relationship entered into because both parties considered it mutually beneficial, would be less a hardship than attempting to fulfill some woman's dream of true love. He disliked hurting people.

Mentally, at least, he'd accepted his late father's mandate, relieved to know he would secure title to the building in which he both lived and made his living. He had plans for the block-long set of storefronts, plans that would benefit both the immediate community and beyond.

So when Amanda, his former fiancée, had shown up with several clearheaded reasons why they should rekindle their engagement, he'd told her about the will. The unromantic marriage directive hadn't fazed her a bit. And he had told himself he had no right to be disappointed by that fact.

A slow creak announced the opening of the bathroom door, and Dean's pulse zoomed. He cast around for something to do so he wouldn't look as if he'd been standing idle, waiting for Rosie, then recognized the absurdity of the thought and remained where he was.

He'd rebroken his engagement to Amanda shortly after seeing Rosie in the market. Without divulging the details, he'd told Amanda that the woman from the market was someone he'd "dated" and was not yet over. She'd questioned him, argued, pointed out that he had to be married in just a couple of months or default on the will, but not once had she tried to hang on to their relationship by saying she loved him. Ending their engagement—again—hadn't been nearly as difficult as it should have been.

It seemed to take an aeon for Rosie to emerge from the bathroom, an aeon during which Dean once again wondered what he was hoping for tonight.

Rosie's desire for a negative result on the test was clear and fervent; how could he hope for anything different?

She entered the hallway, adjusting the strap of her purse securely on her shoulder as she headed toward the living room. Dean's heart pounded like the hooves of a thousand horses.

In her left hand, she carried the test stick like a spoon with an egg on it, moving so cautiously it appeared she was afraid the slightest jostle might tamper with the results.

As she approached, Dean offered a supportive nod.

Rosie looked exhausted, as if she needed a stiff drink or a long vacation. Dark shadows rimmed her eyes, marring the silky skin he remembered so well. He wished he had the right to take her in his arms as he had that night.

Whatever had happened to change her mind about him, his attraction to her had not lessened. He didn't expect it to now. Silently, he vowed to see her smile genuinely at least once before she left tonight. In the meantime, he read the stick she handed him. His breath caught and held.

Instantly, his world calmed as he read the results. The thundering hooves slowed and then grew still in his chest. Every tense muscle released. For the first time in a damned long while, he knew exactly what he wanted, and it was exactly what he was getting.

One thin pink line.

Congratulations, Dean Kingsley. You're going to be a father.

Chapter Four

"You have got to be kidding me." Fletcher Kingsley gaped at his older brother. "You knocked someone up? In a one-night stand? *You?*"

Disbelief and—undeniably—enjoyment mingled in Fletcher's expression.

Dean began seriously to regret coming to his brother for "support." For too long Fletcher had played the badass while Dean had enjoyed a golden-boy image around town. Expecting Fletcher not to gloat now had obviously been unrealistic.

"I'll be damned." Fletch shook his head. "I'd guess this is about the will, but that would *really* be out of character." He narrowed his eyes, scrutinizing his brother closely. "It's over with Amanda, I take it?"

"It was over *before* I knew about the pregnancy."

Fixing one of his sons' lariats, Fletcher worked deftly with the rope while muttering, "Thank God for small favors. That would have been a marriage made in hell."

"Fletcher!" Claire Kingsley emerged from the house, shouldering open the screen door, a tray of refreshments in her hands and a look of gentle admonishment on her pretty face.

As the screen door creaked then slapped shut behind her, Fletcher hopped to his feet, taking the tray while Claire re-positioned a small table next to Dean's chair.

Dean smiled. His brother had struck gold when he'd met the woman who was now his bride of three months. Fletcher was a new man, happy down to his bones.

"I like Amanda," Claire stated as she set out a pitcher of lemonade, glasses and a plate of homemade molasses snaps. "I know she seems chilly at times—"

"Iceland is chilly," her husband interjected, "Amanda could freeze lava."

"Fletcher!" Shaking her head, Claire poured lemonade. "I know for a fact that beneath her defenses, Amanda is a romantic."

Fletcher coughed loudly as he resumed his seat. Dean didn't want to disrespect his sister-in-law, whom he had come to care for deeply, but even he had a hard time reconciling Amanda with *romantic*.

"How do you know?" he asked, accepting a glass of lemonade.

Fletcher winced. "Please don't go there."

Pinching her husband's earlobe while she smiled at her brother-in-law, Claire replied, "Amanda comes to the bakery every couple of days. No matter what else she buys, she always, always gets two strawberry thumbprint cookies. I'm sure those are for her."

Dean looked at Fletcher for clarification. His brother rolled his eyes. "Wait for it."

"We use a heart-shaped cookie cutter and add jam to the dough so the cookies turn pink," Claire explained. "She's feeding the little girl inside her. The one who still dreams of pink hearts and true love."

Dean stared.

Fletcher ate half a molasses snap in one bite. "Claire believes every baked good tells a story."

"It does. Which is why you like bear claws." She put a hand on Fletcher's shoulder. "They sound scary, but inside they're sweet as sugar."

Fletcher, who had indeed sounded scary before being transformed by his wife, grinned. "Can't argue with logic like that." He pulled her close against his side.

"It still doesn't mean I thought Amanda was exactly right for *you*," Claire told Dean. "I can't imagine you spending your life with anyone other than your soul mate, will or no will."

"My current situation doesn't have anything to do with the will." Dean confirmed Fletcher's earlier assessment.

"So who's the mother of our future niece or nephew?" Fletcher's tone was amused, but his gaze turned piercing.

Eight years younger than Dean and raised by a different mother, Fletcher had never exhibited any protective instincts where his older brother was concerned. Yet protectiveness was precisely what Dean saw in the concerned gazes of his family.

"Her name is Rosie," he said. "She works at the library."

"Rosie...Rosemary Jeffers, the new librarian? The boys love her!" Claire exclaimed.

"You had a one-nighter with the new librarian?" Fletcher's frown melted, and he gave a hoot of appreciative laughter. "It figures. Even your indiscretions turn respectable."

"This one hasn't." Irritated and guilt-ridden, Dean downed half the glass of lemonade, wondering whether Rosie had told anyone yet and, if so, what kind of response she'd received.

"Are the two of you getting to know each other better now?" Claire offered him the plate of cookies.

"Not really." He accepted one of the molasses snaps, but had no appetite. His guilt swelled. "I don't even know how she feels about the pregnancy, except that she's scared. We agreed to meet in a couple of days to discuss what we're going to do."

"What are the options?" Fletcher squinted at him.

Dean rubbed his head, mussing the hair that was typically neatly combed. "I'm not certain. I don't know yet how she feels about marriage and kids."

"Meaning she could decide to terminate the pregnancy?"

"No!" Dean glared at his brother, outraged that Fletcher had asked. Then he saw Claire's expression—concerned and compassionate, as if she were a step ahead of him in her understanding of the situation—and realized he had no idea what Rosie was thinking. Could abortion be one of the responses she was considering?

"That's not what you want, then," Fletcher stated.

"No. Hell, no!" Dean realized he was firm on that. "If she doesn't want children…I'll raise the baby."

Fletcher and Claire shared a glance, and Dean could see the bubble above their heads. *Famous last words from the perennial bachelor.*

"Mom! Mom! We need cookies for our fort!"

Dean's nephew Will raced up to the porch, followed swiftly by his younger brother, Orlando.

"I want lemonade!" Orlando clambered up the heavy railing Fletcher had installed after Claire and her children had moved in. "We're invitin' Bigfoot to be in our secret club, so we need a *biiig* glass! Hi, Dad!" Orlando's exuberant rush of words ended in a smacking kiss he planted on Fletcher's lips.

Claire reached for the glasses. "Wow, Mom, that looks delicious. May we have lemonade and cookies, *please?*"

Fletcher raised a brow at his sons, and, smiling sheepishly

at their mother, they rephrased their requests. Claire happily complied, preparing a plate of cookies and three glasses of lemonade—one for Bigfoot.

"We'll see you tomorrow for Free Friday, right, Uncle Dean?" Will asked in his more customary well-mannered way.

"Absolutely, Will. It's a Kingsley tradition." A tradition Fletcher had made up the day he'd met Claire and her children. Realizing she couldn't afford to buy her kids an ice cream, and feeling guilty for the way he'd initially treated the small family, Fletcher had invented Free Fridays at the pharmacy soda fountain—one scoop of ice cream and one topping on the house, every Friday. Though it ate into his profits a bit, Dean had soon made it a regular promotion, open to the public. The benefits—the giddy smiles of kids and their parents lured by ice cream—outweighed his losses.

Fletcher rose to help Claire carry everything to the boys' tree house, and Dean watched the young family progress across the lawn, Will sticking close to his new father's side and Orlando instructing his mother to count as he performed an impressive succession of cartwheels en route to their destination. The fifth member of the family, an enchanting fifteen-month-old named Rosalind, was currently napping inside.

Lucky. That was the word that popped to mind when Dean thought of the family that had been created here on this ranch. Three children who had lost their father now had a man to love and protect them again; a woman who had been shouldering numerous responsibilities on her own had a devoted partner who would lay his life down on her behalf; and a man who formerly had had no life at all now lived as fully as anyone Dean had ever known. Love had made them all whole. Exactly as life should be.

Unlike Fletcher, who had once been the king of cynicism, Dean had always believed that a pure and endless love existed.

His doubts around the topic centered on the disbelief that such a feeling would ever happen to *him*. In thirty-five years he had never lost control of his heart.

Still, as he listened to Claire count cartwheels and Fletcher laugh at his son's antics, Dean acknowledged the firm conviction that a child should be raised in a family. And while "family" could be defined in a variety of ways, his desires were crystal clear: he and Rosie had created a baby, and that baby should turn cartwheels someday with two parents to watch him. Or her.

He stood. He'd intended to give Rosie a couple of days to process their "situation" before he spoke with her again. Bad plan, he realized now. Giving her more time to put a wedge between them would not yield the results he wanted.

And he did know what he wanted. He knew exactly.

Downing the rest of his lemonade as if it were a double shot of courage, he set the glass on the table and walked down the porch steps to say goodbye to his brother, sister-in-law and the boys. He had some business to attend to, and there was no time like the present.

Chapter Five

Rosemary had been back at work for a couple of days when Dean walked into the library. As far as she knew it was the first time he'd been here since she'd started the job in January.

Seated at the reference desk, she watched him stride through the double doors, greeting three people by name before he spotted her. Her heart began to beat too fast and too hard.

He wore his white lab coat and carried a bag from Honey Bea's Bakery. When he stopped in front of the reference desk and plopped the white bag in front of her, she strongly doubted he'd come in to ask whether the library had the latest edition of *Physician's Desk Reference.* She glanced at Circulation, where Abby was replacing a bar code, then back at Dean. *Please do not say the word* pregnant. *Do not say anything about us,* she pleaded silently, *or indicate in any way that there is or ever was an "us," or that I know you as anything other than the friendly neighborhood pharmacist.*

Her too-damn-friendly neighborhood pharmacist.

"Rosie," he greeted.

She grit her teeth. *I have got to tell him not to call me that.*

"Nice to see you again." He spoke as calmly and pleasantly as if the only place they'd ever met was a church coffee hour. Raising his voice slightly, he asked, "I wonder if you could help me find something."

She blinked. He was here as a library patron?

"Quite possibly," she murmured. "What are you look-ing for?" Her trembling fingers poised over the computer keyboard.

Dean leaned forward—way forward—his classic features appearing more handsome the closer he got. He dropped his voice to a whisper. "You." More audibly, he asked, "Do you have the latest Laurence Gonzales novel?" And, softly again, "When do you take lunch?"

"I believe our copy is circulating," she responded loudly to his first question. "Let me check the rest of the system." Her fingers flew across the keyboard. In a low hiss, she told him, "I am not spending my lunch hour with you. This entire library would buzz with gossip." Clicking the mouse three times in rapid succession, she returned to a voice that carried. "Yes, I'm afraid all copies are circulating. Would you like to place a hold?"

"Sounds great," he boomed for anyone nearby to hear. And then quietly, "What kind of hold do you have in mind?"

Rosemary's gaze flew to his.

He winked. "Because I was rather fond of the hold you used when—"

"Shh! Shhhhhh!" She shushed like the classic librarian. Unable to stop herself, Rosemary glanced wildly around, not-ing that her library was beginning to fill with the noontime regulars. When a couple of people looked over, she peeled her puckered lips back in a toothy smile.

Dean turned and smiled, as well. "Hello, Mrs. Covington," he called out, nodding to an older woman who owned more hats than anyone else in Honeyford. Today she had on a short-brimmed blue straw with morning glory and a purple butterfly springing from the wide band. "You look particularly charming today."

The octogenarian beamed, leaving her place in front of the large-print section to join them at the reference desk.

"Good afternoon, Mr. Kingsley. Miss Jeffers."

Some of the older folks in Honeyford preferred a more formal style of address, Rosemary had discovered. Ordinarily she enjoyed conversing with EthelAnne Covington and being swept into the woman's more gracious era, but today she'd give anything to clear the library of all humans. How much simpler life would be if she were left alone with her books! The most complex tome seemed like kid stuff compared to the tangled web of her current circumstances: pregnant and single only two and a half months into her job in a conservative small town.

"Is there anything I can do for you, Mrs. Covington?" she asked, hoping that if she became involved with her customers Dean would disappear.

"Why no, thank you, dear, not at the moment. I came over to speak with Mr. Kingsley, if I may." *Drat.* "I hope I'm not crossing too many boundaries by accosting my pharmacist in the library," she said to Dean with a near-girlish laugh, "but you were my next stop today."

Sensing an opportunity after all, Rosemary stood. On the verge of excusing herself, she felt her wrist caught in a masculine hold. Surprised, she gazed down stupidly at Dean's fingers as they curled around her.

"If you'll wait just a moment, *Ms. Jeffers,*" he said. "I'm not quite finished with my...questions."

To EthelAnne, he inquired graciously, "What can I do for you, dear?"

The elderly woman obviously adored the endearment.

Rosemary's wrist—no, her entire arm—began to feel hot. She needed an avenue of escape *right now.* Dean was practically sitting on her reference desk, holding her arm as if such a gesture were nothing out of the ordinary. Even if EthelAnne didn't think that was odd, someone else was bound to walk by and take notice. Then questions would begin. Questions Rosemary was nowhere near ready to answer.

When she attempted to extricate herself, Dean's casual hold tightened briefly, as if in warning. She considered picking up her stapler and wrapping him on the knuckles. Before she could make her move, his fingers began to lightly stroke the underside of her wrist, away from Mrs. Covington's view. Goose bumps shivered up Rosemary's arm.

Darn him!

"I've just been speaking to Gabrielle Coombs," Mrs. Covington said, blithely unaware of the drama in front of her. "She's on the July Fourth entertainment committee. Lovely young woman, so civic-minded."

"Yes," Dean murmured. His fingertips began to trace tiny circles while Rosemary considered the various ways she could either break free or murder him in full view of her patrons. Unfortunately her brain grew fuzzier with each slow, tantalizing circle.

"I know you're aware that your brother is Grand Marshall of our Honeyford Days Spring Festival," EthelAnne said to Dean. "We're so appreciative that he agreed. What you don't know is that a few of us 'old-timers'—" she laughed as if they really weren't old-timers at all "—in The Betterment of Honeyford Society have written a play depicting Honeyford's history. Since he's the only professional actor we know, we're wondering whether he might agree to perform a role in our theatrical sortie."

Dean's fingers ceased their circles on Rosemary's wrist. "A play," he murmured, frowning. "Uh...my brother isn't a theatrical actor, Mrs. Covington, he was a bull rider and—"

"Oh, but he's very high-profile. The cities of Bend and Sisters draw tourists throughout the year. If Honeyford can accomplish that, every business in town will benefit. And what better way to draw tourists than to offer them special events they can't find anywhere else? I'm quite certain that with the right cast we can pack the community center to the rafters." Her thin fingers fluttered like angel wings toward the ceiling. "And it's no sin to want to win." Her hands came back to rest in pretty-please position. "Will you ask him?"

Rosemary could see Dean struggling with the desire to be of service and the reluctance to approach his brother. She wondered what kind of relationship he had with his family. Who, for that matter, were his family members? She knew nothing important about him.

You know he's a generous lover.

Heat suffused her face seconds after the thought struck. Still, it was true. By the time they'd arrived at the motel, they'd both been almost comically ready to shuck their clothes. She'd been surprised by her own eagerness, though not by Dean's. Weren't most men in a hurry once they'd determined they were going to have sex?

And yet he'd been considerate, unselfish and...romantic. Rosemary wondered whether it was reasonable to call the actions of someone who didn't even know you romantic. Vi had once dated a man who, she said, could look at any woman as if she were the only woman in the world. It wasn't personal. With Dean, everything had felt personal.

Rosemary knew that her mother and sisters would, if consulted, tell her to get her head out of the clouds. The Jeffers women were historically unlucky in love. Rosemary's mother had jettisoned her own husband when her daughters were still wearing footed pajamas. She'd raised her girls to be independent, strong and, above all, realistic. Rosemary's two sisters had never, as far as she knew, believed in Santa Claus, the Tooth Fairy or any story ending in "…and they lived happily ever after." Which was why Rosemary had always felt like a disappointment to her family. She'd once set out cookies for Santa on a little dish she'd set behind a chair so her mother wouldn't see it. It had taken hours to cut out the tiny arrows she'd taped on the floor after everyone else had gone to bed, in the hope that Santa would find his snack. He hadn't. The Tooth Fairy had never taken any of the teeth Rosemary had slipped under her pillow, either, and as for "happily ever after"… These days Rosemary knew where all the fairy tales were shelved in the library, but never again would she count on real life being so accommodating.

"I share your interest in bringing more tourism to Honeyford, Mrs. Covington." Dean smiled gently at the older woman as he prepared to disappoint her. "And I'll help in any way I'm able, but I can't imagine my brother agreeing to—"

"Bridgett Kramer has agreed to sew his costume from scratch! She's an award-winning seamstress, you know," EthelAnne "It's No Sin to Win" Covington interrupted, trying to cut a refusal off at the pass. "Bridgett found a wonderful pattern for an Uncle Sam costume. It even has spats."

"You want Fletcher to play Uncle Sam?"

"Yes, and Ed Fremont will loan us a top hat that Bridgett can decorate"

"A top hat." Rosemary saw the muscles around Dean's mouth twitch. "White beard, too?"

"Of course." EthelAnne looked at Dean with exquisite hope. "You'll ask him, then?"

Dean's smile spread handsomely across his face. Rosemary

knew instantly that he was laughing at himself and his brother, rather than at EthelAnne. She wondered again what kind of family relationships he had. Fun? Casual? She couldn't recall the last time she had simply laughed with her mother or sisters. When they had dinner or got together for holidays, suits and cell phones were the order of the day. She felt herself frowning then saw Dean turn to her. He winked.

That was all—just a quick, sharing-the-joke wink—but Rosemary felt the connection all the way down to her toes. She felt connected, she realized with a jolt, connected to *him*. She didn't even have time to tell herself how absurd that was, or to get her head out of the clouds. Immediately the warm, knee-wobbling feeling spread through her.

She began to feel queasy. It might have been her pregnancy, it might have been fear, but either way Dean was responsible.

"I'll speak to him at my first opportunity," Dean promised, eliciting a clap of delight from EthelAnne, whose nails, Rosemary noted dimly, were painted a hopeful peony-pink. "May I ask you for a favor now, Mrs. Covington?"

"Why, certainly!" EthelAnne's eyes sparkled with eagerness.

"Do you think you could help convince this lovely lady to have lunch with me?" Rosemary's eyes widened as he gestured to her, his eyes flashing with bald interest. "I haven't had a chance yet to welcome our new librarian to town, and as president of the Chamber of Commerce, I consider it my responsibility."

There might have been a couple of decades between Ethel-Anne Covington and her last date, but she didn't miss Dean's true intent. She looked between the two of them, clearly delighted, and Rosemary felt her anxiety spike to out-and-out panic.

"That's not necessary." She held up a hand, shaking her

head at the same time. "We're a library—we don't deal in any kind of commerce, so it's not your responsibility—"

EthelAnne laughed. "Oh, dear, you're very literal. Dean is one of Honeyford's most conscientious citizens. I'm sure he won't sleep a wink until he's performed his civic duty."

The laugh lines around Dean's mouth deepened, but he raised his brows innocently. Rosemary's brain scrambled for a way out and latched on to "too much work" as an excuse, but she never got to utter it.

Irene Gould, who led the book club that met in the conference room every Tuesday evening, approached the reference desk and exclaimed, "How lovely! Three of my favorite people in one location!"

Rosemary winced. Why did everyone sound as if they were speaking through megaphones today? "May I help you, Irene?" she said quickly. "Do you have a question?" *Because this is the reference desk, after all, not a singles' bar.*

"We were just convincing Miss Jeffers to—"

Oh, for the love of heaven...

"—allow Mr. Kingsley to accompany her to lunch. As a gesture of welcome." EthelAnne filled Irene in on the topic du jour.

Behind purple-framed glasses, Irene's blue eyes rapidly assessed the situation. "Wonderful idea! The diner has a sublime mulligatawny soup today."

Dean reached for the white bag he'd brought with him. "Actually I picked up sandwiches at Honey Bea's." This time when he made eye contact with Rosie his expression was more sympathetic than humor-filled or victorious.

Less than ten minutes later, Rosemary and Dean were walking side by side down C Street.

"I know I should apologize," he admitted, his voice deep and smooth, "but I can't claim true repentance."

The late-winter day was crisp, but sunny. Rosemary shoved

her hands in the pockets of the thick periwinkle cardigan she'd grabbed on her way out of the library.

"I was under the impression that Honeyford is a conservative town," she complained. "Doesn't anyone care that you were *engaged* just a few days ago?"

"Very few people knew about my engagement, Rosie. We hadn't officially announced it yet, and Amanda lives and works in Salem. She doesn't particularly care for small-town life, so generally we got together in the city. The night you saw us in the market was one of the rare exceptions when she came here."

Their shoes crunched along the gravel that substituted for a sidewalk on a portion of the street.

"Were you planning to move to Salem?" Rosemary asked. If he had, she might never have met him again, even after she'd discovered she was pregnant with his baby. Would that have been better?

They crunched a few more steps, and Dean responded, "We were going to commute to be together on weekends."

He was staring straight ahead, frowning. His former marriage plans were none of her business. Zero. Not a bit. But she'd been married to a man who had worked so much that they'd had a weekend marriage even though they'd lived in the same house seven days a week. They had lost their connection to each other years before the marriage had ended. She wished she'd seen it sooner.

"Marriage has to take place seven days a week," she said, "wherever you are. But it would be a lot harder if you weren't even in the same town. Everyone takes for granted that love will get them through the hard times." She shook her head. "It won't. Love comes and goes—that's natural. If the commitment to an ideal isn't there—" Hearing the fervor in her voice, Rosemary stopped. She felt Dean's gaze on her.

"How long were you married?" he asked quietly.

Panic gurgled through her. Her marriage was too private, too confusing and too much a failure to discuss. "Who said I was?"

Dean's hand grasped her elbow, firmly stopping her when she would have kept walking. He faced her, and she stared at his chest, but he wasn't having any of that, either. Tucking a finger under her chin, he raised her face.

His expression was serious, direct. "One thing we can be with each other is honest," he said. "That's one thing we *should* to be. Our child ought to have parents who talk to each other, at the very least."

The mention of *their* child reminded Rosie that something much larger than her feelings or his was at stake. For better or worse, she had to find a way to get along with this person that one aberrant, passionate night had permanently affixed in her orbit. Still, there had to be boundaries.

"I honestly don't want to discuss my marriage," she said, meaning what she said without saying it meanly. "Not right now."

He wasn't happy with her answer, but he accepted it. "All right. I'm a willing listener if you change your mind." He let go of her chin, glancing at the sky and looking, she thought, like the leader of a lion pride, testing the air to see what the pride's next move should be. When he glanced back to her, she had to give herself a mental shake.

"I took a long lunch break today," he told her. "Half an hour to convince you to join me, and an hour for us to eat and talk." The appealing, self-mocking smile curved his lips again. "I figure we both have about fifty-five minutes left. My place is close by, or it might be warm enough to sit in the park."

"Park," she chose immediately, thinking that it had taken her a decade of marriage to accept that men didn't like to sit and talk. Just her luck that she'd had a one-night stand with a man who wanted to get chatty. At least if they went to the park, where there might be other people enjoying the spring day, she'd feel safer. After days—and nights—deliberating, she had decided how she wanted to handle her pregnancy and his involvement with the baby, assuming he insisted on any. In a public place his reaction would necessarily be tempered, and that was a good thing. Because she was darn sure he wasn't going to like her plan one bit.

Chapter Six

Dean had never in his life wanted anything as much as he wanted to break down the wall Rosemary Jeffers had erected around herself…and his baby.

The child growing inside her was his, and whatever else might be right or wrong about their relationship took a backseat to that singular fact. A month ago, engaged to Amanda for reasons more practical than idealistic, he'd considered a future without children and had thought he might be fine focusing on his business, his plans to open a community health cooperative and spending time with his new niece and nephews. His life would be full enough.

Now fatherhood was an imminent reality. That changed everything, including his approach toward Rosie. Getting past her defenses wasn't an option: it was a necessity.

"The park is up Fifth Street," he said, pointing as they approached Main. Deliberately, he tempered his ground-eating strides to more closely match the steps she took—short and reluctant, as if she were shuffling to her own guillotine. "It's got covered picnic tables and a gazebo."

"I know. I walk by it when I go to work."

"Speaking of work, is that what brought you to Honeyford?"

"Yes."

When she declined to elaborate, Dean persisted. "I'm sure library jobs are hard to come by in this economy, but even so there are people who would resist living in a town of under two thousand. Particularly young, beautiful, single women."

He saw her thin, dark brows arch in surprise, watched a pink blush stain her ivory cheeks, and felt both pleased and annoyed that someone as lovely as she would be surprised to hear a man refer to her as beautiful.

He put a hand beneath her elbow as they traversed Main, but released her once they were safely across.

"Were you coming from another small town?" he asked, determined to discover, one way or another, how she had lived—and with whom—prior to moving to Central Oregon. And prior to showing up at Tavern on the Highway.

"I grew up in Portland," Rosie revealed hesitantly. "I've never lived anywhere but a city."

Dean whistled. "From Portland to Honeyford. Kind of like switching from triple-shot espresso to decaf."

Rosie laughed, and he liked the sound of it. "So you stayed in Portland after school," he prompted. "Where did you meet the women who were at the Tavern with you?"

"We went to high school together."

"It says a lot that you've remained friends through the years. Are you pretty loyal in general?"

Rosie seemed to relax a bit as they moved away from Main Street. She considered his question. "Yes. I'm loyal." She slanted a glance at him. "And, no, I am not going to discuss my marriage with you, and, yes, I know that's where you're going with this."

He laughed. "Still, the least you can do is tell me whether you were a free agent the night we met. Because I'm concerned that *you* might have compromised *me*."

"*You're* concerned?"

"I already told you that you have nothing to worry about. Care to put my mind at ease? I'd hate to go to my grave thinking I was 'the other man.'"

She shook her head, appearing partly amused, and partly *be*mused. "Reassuring my one-night stand," she murmured. "You boy toys are a lot more high maintenance than I knew."

"It's hard not knowing where you stand. We're sensitive that way." Call him old-fashioned, he liked being reminded that he was her first and, so far, only fling. "So?" He waggled his brows, inviting her answer.

"You can sleep like a baby tonight. I was a completely free agent."

A knot of tension in Dean's chest began to loosen at the news. "On the rebound from anyone?"

"Dean…" she warned, still prickly about getting personal despite the fact that they'd already been about as personal as a couple could get. He decided not to back down.

"It's that darn sensitivity issue again. How about you humor me this one time?"

"I have a feeling that humoring you 'one time' is like handing a six-year-old one M&M and expecting him not to ask for another."

Laughter dissolved the rest of the knot. "You're right."

"I wasn't on the rebound. I hadn't been in a relationship at all for a couple of years. And that's all I'm saying," she hastened to add. "So move on now."

"Okay. We'll talk about neutral things until we get to the park."

"The park is only a block away."

"Yeah." He clucked his tongue regretfully. "That's the problem with small towns. The geography makes a lengthy neutral discussion almost impossible."

She cocked her head, looking adorable, he decided. Finally she merely shook her head at him, but he noticed her lips twitching.

When they reached the park, they had a choice between having their lunch at the picnic tables or in the gazebo. Rosie chose the gazebo, a fact he filed away for future use. Gazebos were, after all, pure small-town romance.

Dean couldn't claim a wealth of experience in the realm of romancing a woman. Amanda had been decidedly "anti-artifice," as she referred to the trappings of courtship. His sister-in-law's appraisal that Amanda was a romantic at heart because she had a penchant for pink cookies didn't jive a bit with what he'd experienced of his former fiancée, but now he wondered whether he hadn't tried hard enough to turn their engagement into more of a courtship. The motivation hadn't been there, on either side.

With Rosie, the motivation was a continuous hum.

He couldn't look at her without remembering the sight of her in bed, the feel of her beneath him and the half surprised, half uncontrollable sounds of her pleasure.

That's what he wanted again. He'd wanted it about every fifteen minutes since that night. He wanted it right now, before lunch, in the gazebo if necessary and with as little foreplay as possible.

And then he'd romance her. He'd give her all the hearts, flowers, candlelight and whatever else a woman wanted until the thought of him, of *them,* filled her mind the way it had been filling his. And then—

God willing, sex again.

Sitting demurely on the gazebo's curved bench, Rosie folded her hands on her lap.

Dean loosened the tie he'd worn to work. *You are lusting after the mother of your child.*

Seemed like a good sign.

He sat beside her, leaving enough space between them for her to feel comfortable. He had always, after all, been a polite man. Self-control had never been a chore for him; it came naturally.

He wanted to push her cardigan aside and dip his hand into the loose neckline of her dress, remembering exactly what he'd find inside. And how she had felt, cupped in his palm. And how damn perfect she'd looked to him.

Quickly, he unrolled the white bakery bag. "Turkey?" His voice sounded as if he'd dragged his vocal chords across sandpaper. Sweat popped out along his upper lip. He wiped it away, clearing his throat. "It's warm today."

Rosie dragged the edges of her sweater closer together. "I'm a little chilly." Taking the sandwich he offered her, she gave him a weak smile. "This looks good. Thank you."

"My pleasure. My sister-in-law works at Honey Bea's." He passed her a napkin and a bottle of sweetened iced tea. "She's hoping to become a full partner this year."

"I've been in the bakery once or twice." Delicately his lunch mate peeled the plastic wrap from a thick, soft roll Dean's brother had dubbed The Rozzy Roll in honor of his toddler daughter, who loved to gnaw them until they were paste. Rosie smiled ruefully. "Generally I try to stay out of bakeries. Also ice-cream parlors and candy stores. I have a runaway sweet tooth."

"Your figure hasn't suffered." He squelched an urge to leer. "Take my word for it."

She ducked her head briefly, making it impossible to gauge

her reaction then said, "I'm going to have to be more careful than ever now that I'm—"

Abruptly she cut herself off, as if refusing to discuss the situation with him would make it less real, or would make him less a part of it.

"Pregnant," he finished for her. Polite or no, he by-God wasn't going to let her skirt the issue. If he did, she'd avoid him until it was time for her to push his baby out.

"I'll remember that you're pregnant, Rosie, whether you mention it or not." Though there was no one nearby to over-hear, he spoke quietly, intently, declaring the intimacy that linked them more loudly than if he'd shouted. "And I do recall…in detail…how you got that way. I remember every time I look at you." Seeing her eyes grow big and round, he hammered home one final point. "Eat. We Kingsleys love a good meal."

He could tell by her expression that she got the drift: this baby was going to be a Kingsley, and he was going to be a very present father. He hadn't considered the day-to-day reality of that nor had he considered any alternatives, but now that he'd spoken he knew exactly where he stood. The only question worth contemplating was whether they were going to parent together or apart.

And, what he was going to do about the damned will.

Looking away, though he wanted nothing more than to crush her to him and see if she tasted as good as she had that night, he concentrated on unwrapping the sandwich instead of the woman. The hunger in his stomach was weak and puny compared to another, more pressing appetite.

All his adult life, Dean had prided himself on being a gentleman. Animals reacted from instinct; human beings used reason to control their behavior. Fletcher had taken the op-posite tack for his first twenty-eight years, generally acting rashly and claiming he left the thinking to Dean. For the first time, Dean envied his younger brother's lack of caution.

The muscles throughout his midsection clenched. Controlling himself with effort, he took a bite of turkey with avocado and Havarti, but his favorite sandwich was tasteless today.

"I have been giving a great deal of thought to our…situation." The voice that came from his right was soft and hesitant, almost as if Rosie were speaking to herself.

At least she said "our" situation, he told himself, swallowing the bite of sandwich and turning toward her fully. "And?"

Her fingers gripped the sandwich. "What you said before— about this town being too small to have a neutral conversation—I know you were being facetious, but it's true in a way. Honeyford's not tiny, but two people with jobs as public as ours are bound to the object of gossip if someone finds out about…"

"Our situation," he supplied wryly.

"Yes."

"Mmm-hmm. I'd say it's more a matter of *when* they find out, not *if.*" He watched her closely, his breath held, feeling clear as a bell that he'd never asked a more important question or waited for a more seminal answer. "Wouldn't you?"

She pressed her lips together, taking time before she answered, and he felt as if he were hanging from the edge of a cliff, waiting for someone either to pull him to safety or pry his fingers loose, one by one.

"If I can find another job," she said, "we might not have to discuss it with anyone for the time being. It could be between the two of us while we figure out the details."

"Another job where?" he asked, hearing the tension in his voice.

"The Tacoma Public Library is looking for someone."

"Tacoma." Dean frowned. "Washington."

She picked at her sandwich, pulling out the tiniest piece of turkey, chewing carefully and swallowing before she explained, "Tacoma is a much larger city. No one there will care if a librarian is single and pregnant."

"Ah." He nodded, setting aside his sandwich. "Right. Because we're pretty provincial here. Burned a witch just last week."

She didn't smile. Just as well. He wasn't feeling particularly good-humored, either.

"I mean that I don't know anyone there, so I won't have to explain anything," she said, her voice stronger now. "And the baby won't have to worry about being the object of curiosity, or worse. When I interviewed for my job, I was told I'd be working with the community a great deal, and it was made abundantly clear that a large sector of that community is conservative." Dean opened his mouth, but she overrode him. "I don't mean 'conservative' as in 'I'd better hide all my copies of *Catcher in the Rye*.' But I was asked how I felt about stocking an abundance of G-rated books. In large print."

He frowned, but Rosie only shrugged. "A return to old-fashioned values was one of the things that appealed to me about moving to this town." She slid him a glance that was both wry and regretful. "I didn't get off to a great start. With regard to the old-fashioned values, I mean."

Dean felt a tiny, figurative knife stick him in the gut. He was the indiscretion she regretted.

"I have friends and family in Portland," Rosie continued.

"Isn't Portland several hours from Tacoma?"

"Only three."

"And Portland is three hours from Honeyford, so I'd have a six-hour drive one way to see my child," Dean pointed out, not even mentioning seeing her at this point. "There's no easy way to fly in, either." She started to respond, but this time he overrode her. "But putting the issue of visitation aside for the time being, you're proposing to move to a city where you don't know anyone, when you're on the brink of one of the biggest changes in your life."

"I told you, I have family—"

"Three hours from Tacoma. Right." Controlling his mounting frustration, Dean, too, set his sandwich aside, abandoning the notion of a friendly picnic. "Listen, Rosie—"

"No one calls me, Rosie. I meant to tell you in the library."

He had a clear memory of her introducing herself as "Rosie." *Rosie Jo,* to be exact. Noting the spreading blush on cheeks the color of vanilla ice cream, he had to smile. "That night really was an anomaly for you, wasn't it?"

"I've been cautious my entire life." She wagged her head, raising a hand to swipe at the tears that were spilling over her lashes. "And obviously I was right to be careful. One misstep and now both of our lives are in complete turmoil. I don't even understand how it happened." He quirked a brow, and her blush deepened. "I know *how.* But I've been wracking my brain—" she sniffled loudly "—and I can't remember *not* using a condom." She looked at him in question, biting her lower lip.

Immediately, his groin tightened. He wanted to soothe that worried lower lip with his own mouth. He couldn't help it: he chuckled, drawing a surprised and resentful look from her. "Sorry, but when I think about that night—which I find myself doing frequently, by the way—condoms are hardly ever the first things that come to mind." Reaching into the bakery bag, Dean pulled out a napkin, but rather than handing it to her, he brought the makeshift tissue to her nose and dabbed lightly.

When she grabbed the napkin to do the job herself, it didn't surprise him. Somehow, in some way, she had been hurt, and he was willing to bet that a man had done the deed. *You nearly messed her up for anyone else, buddy. Nearly.*

Bending over her dark, curly head while she delicately blew her nose, he murmured, "So are condoms really all you think about when you remember that night? When you remember us?"

She gasped so hard, he was afraid she might inhale the napkin. He chose not to relent.

"There is an us, you know. Like it or not, what we started that night is something that owns us both now. Two people, one cause. And, like it or not, passion made that baby you're refusing to feed. So, like it or not, I do care whether you eat. I care where my baby is going to live and how easy or difficult it's going to be to get to him. And, I care that that single night in the motel was the best sex I've ever had. In my life. Bar none. You may be over it, *Rosie,* but I'm not. Not by a long shot."

He sat up straight, reached for his sandwich again and winked at her as he took a bite.

Her eyes were wide and troubled; her soft, plump mouth formed a huge O. A pulse throbbed visibly in her neck, the rhythm reminding him more of a marimba band than a heartbeat.

Yep. He'd made his point.

"Your one-night stand lives in the same town you do, and you were together when you found out you were pregnant even though you hadn't seen each other since that night?" Daphne recapped what Rosemary had just told her, her sweet voice rising in disbelief.

"Yes," Rosemary said, trapping the cordless phone between her shoulder and ear while she rummaged through her kitchen pantry, looking for dinner.

Confused, nervous and tense as piano wire since seeing Dean earlier in the day, she had finally decided to break her silence about the pregnancy. After giving brief—very brief—consideration to phoning her mother or one of her sisters, she had decided to lean on Daphne, the only one of her friends so baby crazy that news of a pregnancy, no matter how it had come about, would be received with joyous anticipation.

"Do you feel any different?" Daphne asked with keen interest. "Do you feel pregnant?"

"I'm hungry all the time." She shoved three baked BBQ potato chips into her mouth, grabbed another handful before she made herself roll up the bag then reached for peanut-butter-stuffed pretzels.

"Are you having cravings?"

"Yeah." The potato chips did a quick disappearing act. "I'm craving food." Biting the tip off the pretzel, Rosemary sucked out the candylike nut butter. "When I'm not throwing up. I hate throwing up. But I'm dizzy and nauseous every morning the second I open my eyes. It doesn't go away until late afternoon, and then I'm ravenous the rest of the night."

"Poor baby." Daphne murmured. "What does your doctor say?"

"I haven't seen one yet. I'm going this Friday for the first time. I found an ob-gyn in Bend. That's over an hour from here, which should minimize the likelihood of anyone seeing me and realizing what's going on. Then if I get the job in Tacoma, I can move before I'm showing, and nobody has to know."

After a brief pause, Daphne commented, "I can't believe anyone would really care in this day and age. And you said Honeyford has almost two thousand people, right?"

"That's what *he* said," Rosemary grumbled darkly.

"You could probably keep it private until you're showing, if you really want to," Daphne soothed then emitted her adorable laugh, confessing, "If it were me, I'd get a Baby On Board maternity shirt and start wearing it while I was still a size six. I'd want everyone to know."

Trying to decide between mac and cheese or sardines with mayonnaise and pickle relish on rye, Rosemary made a face into the phone. "I've never been a size six. Do macaroni and cheese and sardines go together?" She was met with silence. "Daphne?"

"I'm sorry. I just threw up a little. Hey, maybe you're superhungry because you're having twins! Are there any twins in your family?"

Rosemary froze with the box of pasta in her hand. "Not on my mother's side. I have no idea about my father's."

"You should ask your mother."

"Great. Now I think *I* just threw up a little." The suggestion that she should consult with Maeve Jeffries about any aspect of this pregnancy temporarily killed Rosemary's runaway appetite. "I doubt my mother knows anything about my father's family. She used to refer to him as The Donor, and she didn't even say it in a derogatory way. She simply didn't see him as essential to our daily lives in any way. When I'd ask her about him, she'd look totally mystified and answer, 'I don't recall, Rosemary.'" Her best friends had met her mother and sisters and understood that she had not grown up conventionally. Still, she hadn't discussed her family in a while. Frowning, she replaced the box of pasta, exhausted suddenly. "My parents must be the only two people on the planet capable of bringing three children into the world without having a single memorable conversation."

Daphne, who had the kind of relationship with her dad that every fatherless little girl dreamed of, responded with her customary quiet compassion. "I'm sorry, sweetie." Then in a tone equally caring, she nudged, "I bet you want something very different for your daughter."

Whomp. As if they were playing verbal dodge ball, Daphne's comment socked Rosemary right in the gut. It was the one hit she couldn't outrun.

"Maybe I'm having a boy," she mumbled, but she knew the sex of the baby didn't matter. She'd been tagged.

It seemed to take great effort to reach the banquette in her kitchen. Sinking heavily into the cushioned seat, she gazed through fluttering white eyelit café curtains. The street was so peaceful this time of evening. This town was everything she'd dreamed of as a girl when she was growing up in the city.

"I'm scared," she whispered.

"I know." Daphne, who was a legal secretary, but should have been a therapist, asked with no judgment in her tone, "How did you get pregnant? It's a little confusing, given that he's a pharmacist and you're an educated woman. I mean, did the pill fail and the condom broke?"

"I haven't been on birth control in two years. And..." Rosemary hesitated, knowing how utterly irresponsible, immature and downright reckless she was going to sound. "I think we forgot to use the condom at one point."

"At one point? How many times that night did you, um, need a condom, if you don't mind my asking?

Rosemary closed her eyes. "Four. But I think time number three was the problem."

Daphne hooted. "Rosemary Josephine Jeffers!"

"I know, I know!" Her forehead lowering all the way to the wood table, Rosemary groaned. "It was a crazy night. It seemed to exist in its own cosmos." She shook her head against the cool wood. "I sound like I'm seventeen on prom night. Except that I was a lot smarter on prom night. I stayed with the group."

Sitting up, she gazed at two deer picking their way across her front lawn. The does' skinny legs raised and lowered with a kind of slow-motion military precision. Having their evening feed before they moved to the beds they made deeper in the pines around Honeyford, the deer would sleep for only a couple of hours at a time, their instinct for survival dictating that they never get too comfortable. Smart deer.

"The worst part is I wasn't paying close enough attention," Rosemary said, "because I felt this…trust when I was with him."

"Why is trusting him the worst part?"

"Because I didn't know him. Because he picked me up in a bar. Because he's a man, and I could have been any woman. Take your pick."

"Hmm. He didn't look at you like you could be any woman. He looked at you like he was…smitten."

Rosemary's emotions responded instantly, before her mind could overrule the reaction. A coil of pleasure sprang up from low in her belly, sending out frissons of electric longing. So much for her survival instinct.

No matter how she'd been raised, no matter how much she'd learned from her own experience or from her mother and sisters' fretful we-told-you-so's after her marriage imploded, she returned over and over to dreams of white picket fences and forever. Her sisters might be slightly rigid in their approach to life, but at least they stayed away from the kind of pain Rosemary apparently courted.

"I should have phoned Vi," she said. "She'd have been cynical. She'd have reminded me what happened the last time I trusted a man." Pain choked her voice to a whisper.

"Yes, she'd have said that. And she'd have told you that deep down men will never want the same things as women, so we should cut the poor sods some slack and use them like the toys they were intended to be. But you didn't phone Vi," Daphne pointed out. "What does your pharmacist/boy toy want to do about the baby?"

"He wants to be involved."

"How involved?"

Rosemary stood and paced to the living room, where she had no idea what to do with herself. She was so tired, she wanted to crawl into bed and so restless she thought perhaps she should go for a run. "When I told him I was considering moving to Tacoma, he said to let him know as soon as I'd made up my mind so he could start looking for employment there."

Daphne's soft intake of breath spoke volumes. "Wow. All right, don't take this the wrong way, but that's more than your family would do. It's more than your friends *could* do, Rosemary. Is he a genuinely nice guy? Because that night he seemed like a genuinely nice guy."

Rosemary halted her pacing in front of her fireplace, fingering the smooth river rock as she tried to steady her thoughts, which flashed immediately to Dean's eyes—so attentive and penetrating—and to his voice, the timbre rich with humor or deep and strong and sober as he set the ground rules for dealing with each other.

"He insists on open lines of communication," she told Daphne. "He said that if nothing else we should be honest with each other."

"Oh, my. How did that feel?" Daphne knew that Neil's dishonesty had left Rosemary with a wound that no amount of emotional suturing seemed to close all the way. "On your birthday you said you wouldn't have a relationship again until you met a completely honest man."

A dull throb filled Rosemary's temples. "Yeah, and Ginger said I'd never date again if that was my criteria."

They fell silent. Daphne had been hurt plenty by men who took one look at her perfect face and Pussycat Doll figure and were willing to tell her anything in order to start a relationship they had little intention of finishing. Daphne was a diehard romantic who had fallen hard more than once, dreaming of "forever." She'd been hurt plenty, and this past New Year's had resolved to be celibate until she heard the words "You may kiss your bride." Rosemary figured that not even Daphne would suggest she should trust a man simply because he *claimed* to value honesty and communication.

But if he values communication, what was up with that engagement of his?

"Remember when we were in high school and had to carry dolls and diaper bags everywhere for Health Ed?" Daphne's voice was soft and reminiscent.

"And we had to set a timer that woke us up every two hours for an entire weekend." Rosemary nodded at the river rock.

"Half the class didn't even complete the assignment. Vi left the baby in her backpack."

Rosemary smiled. "I remember. She said it needed a quiet place to nap."

"Right." Daphne's sweet giggle reached across the miles. "You and I were the only ones who never got tired of it." More seriously she pointed out, "You used to want a family more than anything. We've talked about the guy. The one thing I haven't heard you mention yet is whether you're happy about the baby."

Tears sprang to Rosemary's eyes. Guilt and regret swelled inside her. "I try not to think about the baby," she confessed in a miserable whisper. "I don't want to let myself. Oh, Daphne, I never, ever imagined I'd be a single mother. It makes me so sad to think about it."

"I know." Daphne's understanding made it feel as if she were in the same room. "It doesn't have to feel the way it did when you were growing up, though. You're completely different from Maeve."

Emotion made it difficult for Rosemary to speak, so she nodded into the phone.

"Right now you're frightened because you see yourself

repeating your parents' choices," Daphne said, still with the utmost kindness. "But if Dean wants to be involved, and if he's a reasonable man, maybe you could find a way to work him into your and the baby's life—peacefully. Couldn't you, Rosemary?"

Turning from the fireplace, Rosemary plodded to the downstairs bathroom, wiping the mascara from beneath her eyes. "I have no idea how to make that work, Daph. In my world, there's no precedent for peaceful shared parenting." She plucked a tissue from a box on the counter. "The Jeffers women take the praying-mantis approach."

Daphne laughed. "Well, then your choice is clear—either you set a new precedent or you bite his head off."

Rosemary produced a watery laugh. "Can I think that over and get back to you?"

Chapter Seven

Rosemary had allowed Dean Kingsley to call the shots at their last meeting. In the two days since, she had arrived at a couple of critical decisions, and she was determined that their next meeting be on her terms. She intended to be reasonable, clear and calmly unmovable in her stance.

The best-laid plans...

"Oh, my God, what do you think you're doing?" she whispered fiercely when she came upon him in one of the library's nonfiction aisles—Women's Health, to be exact—holding a copy of *What to Expect When You're Expecting*.

"Browsing," he answered, a slow smile spreading over his face as he turned toward her. "You look great in pink."

Nonplussed, she stared mutely for several seconds then came to and stabbed her finger at the book. "What are you doing with *that?*"

"I'm going to check it out." He tapped the cover. "I hear it's essential reading for pregnancy."

Darting her gaze around the immediate area, she grabbed Dean's arm and tugged him around the back end of the aisle. "Are you crazy? You cannot check that book out!"

"Is it on hold?"

"Very funny." She held out her hand. "Give it to me."

"Sorry, you'll have to get your own copy." One chestnut brow rose. "Unless you want to read it together. I might be open to that."

She thought at first that he was being glib, but the oceanic gaze that settled into hers was alarming in its authenticity, and a lightening bolt seemed to explode in her chest.

"You used to want a family like Vi wants to be CEO of Neiman Marcus," Daphne had reminded her before they'd hung up last night.

Her heart hammered unevenly. She didn't expect to have a *family* anymore, not in the traditional sense, and she was okay with that, or would be. That was one of the conclusions she'd come to last night.

Holding out her hand, she said, "Give me the book so I can check it out *privately,* and I'll bring it to you."

"When?"

"Tonight."

"Where?"

What were the chances he'd agree to meeting in Bend, an hour away?

"Try not to overthink this one, Rosie."

She glanced around. "Would you please call me Rose*mary,* like everyone else?"

He narrowed his eyes, considering. "We can talk about it later. You *may* be able to persuade me. Time and place?"

"Seven o'clock. At...Tavern on the Highway," she decided quickly.

"Sentimental."

"We're less likely to be spotted there."

"Practical *and* sentimental."

"May I have your library card, please?"

He reached for his wallet. "Okay, but just so you know, I usually share this only with women who are serious about me. I'll make an exception in your case. This time." He handed over the card. "Before I give it to you again, I'll need a definite commitment."

He arrived at the tavern early since it was Saturday, and he wanted to scope out a table as far as possible from the music and the beer. Dean found her choice of meeting locations telling.

As he pushed toward the bar, wading through the noise and memories, his mood plunged to something dull and dark around the edges. For days, ever since he'd seen Rosie…Rosemary…again—and certainly since the discovery that she was pregnant—he'd expected to rediscover the woman he'd met here in December. He'd felt sure that somewhere beneath the distance and the denial, she still existed.

Now, before she even arrived, he felt hope waning. Being here afforded him a visceral reminder of the feelings he'd had that night. He remembered Rosie Jo in vivid detail.

Rosemary Jeffers appeared to be someone else altogether.

Wedging between the patrons at the bar, he placed his order. "Obsidian Stout and—" Damn, what would she want now that she couldn't have alcohol? "Scratch the stout. Orange juice on the rocks. Two."

Waiting for the drinks, he let his gaze wander out to the dance floor. About fifteen people were line dancing, but in his mind he saw a slow dance, with two bodies moving in perfect unison, getting to know the feel of each other and the smell and the sweetness. He saw a woman with no reserve looking up at him, her lovely eyes deep and hazel and promising.

His body tightened with longing. He'd fallen for a one-night fantasy. He felt like a girl.

"Two OJs." The bartender placed the drinks in front of him. "Sip slowly."

Dean set off to locate a table, but hadn't taken more than a couple of steps when he heard an familiar, accent-laced, "Hey, *compadre*."

"Alberto." Balancing the tumblers of juice on one palm, Dean clasped his friend's hand. "I haven't seen you in a couple of months. Where've you been?"

"I was in Medford, working with *un hombre muy rico*—" he laughed "—to renovate a building." Alberto's black eyes glowed with the quiet humor that was characteristic of him. "Old brick and exposed pipes, like your building. I learned a lot that will help us." Holding a drink Dean knew was non-alcoholic, he elbowed his old friend. "I hear you're engaged now. In the nick of time. *Sí?*" he asked, his interest keen. "So the building is guaranteed."

Discomfort engulfed Dean. Alberto knew about the will Dean's father had left and about the marriage codicil that gave Dean ownership of half a block of storefronts on Honeyford's Main Street, as long as he married within the specified period of time and remained so for two years.

Alberto wanted Dean to acquire ownership of the property as much as Dean wanted it.

"When do we get started?"

Alberto's skin was the color of fine leather, lined with more care than a forty-year-old man should have confronted.

Dean met the Flores family eight years ago, when Alberto came to the pharmacy, inquiring about medicine for his daughter, Adelina. The girl had been ill for several days, treated only with home remedies due to the family's financial circumstances and a lack of education regarding health care and the state health-care system.

After listening to Alberto's nervous recitation of the young girl's symptoms, Dean insisted that his father visit the Flores family at their home. Victor Kingsley hospitalized Adelina for pneumonia immediately, but the medical intervention occurred too late.

Accompanying his father to the Flores home, Dean watched the beautiful cinnamon-skinned girl, her ribbons of ebony hair dampened with perspiration, full lips parted with the effort to breathe while her mother whispered to her in Spanish. The walls of the Flores house were cracked, patched, he had later learned, again and again by Alberto himself when he could afford the materials. The girl lay in the family's only bed; Alberto had been sleeping on the floor. Dean had felt a sharp, furious frustration as he realized the Flores family and their neighbors availed themselves of medical care only at the last possible moment—and even then, generally only for their children.

At Dr. Victor Kingsley's stoic insistence, Adelina was transported to the pediatric unit of a medical center in Bend, where she died before her tenth birthday. The Flores family was destroyed.

Alberto began drinking. Eventually his wife sought her solace with family in Mexico, and Dean found the gentle man living on the street.

"Let's have lunch this week, and I'll tell you what's going on," Dean prevaricated, hoping that by the end of the week he might have some ideas about how to salvage his plans to put a low-cost, bilingual health-care clinic in the building his father had owned.

Dean had driven Alberto to his first AA meeting. In the following months, they had spoken frequently. The idea for Clinica Adelina Community Health Care was born in these conversations and out of Alberto's desperate need to deal with what he perceived as his terrible failure.

"It looks as if another grant is going to come through." Dean watched pleasure spark in Alberto's eyes and felt some guilt about not disclosing the demise of his engagement, a crucial component in making the dream of a clinic come true. Perhaps they could find some other venue, someone willing to donate the space....

The music changed, and Alberto grinned. "Time for line dancing." He gestured to the glasses in Dean's hand. "You here with your *novia?*"

After some hesitation, Dean answered, "No. I'm expecting a friend."

They agreed to be in touch the following week, and Alberto moved on. Dean found a table far from the dance floor and waited. Precisely at 7:00 p.m., Rosie walked in.

She wore a camel-hair coat over the same skirt and sweater outfit she'd had on earlier. Curls the color of coffee beans framed her face and bounced thickly on her shoulders. She took several steps into the tavern then stopped and looked around, searching for him.

Dean's hand came halfway up then stopped. Every time he saw her, a smile rose from his chest, but she appeared as tight-laced and miserable as she had since December, and his optimism fell another notch.

One night and a baby did not turn two strangers into a couple. As much as he wanted to rediscover the woman who had smiled like the sun and whose starry eyes had sparkled with humor, it was time to admit that he may have been mistaken about her. It wouldn't be the first time that a man in his family had fallen for the wrong woman.

Was he like his father? Victor had been three-times unlucky in love. By most accounts, he had loved Dean's mother, but she had passed on when her marriage was still young and her son a mere child. There was no telling whether that marriage would have lasted. Dean barely remembered his mother, but he knew that emotional availability had not been his father's greatest gift.

Victor's second marriage, to Fletcher's mother, could only be termed a tragedy, though it had begun with the anticipation of rebuilding a family. Jule Kingsley had been more mercurial than the Oregon weather. A delight one moment, incomprehensibly distraught the next, she had harbored pain and secrets that had nearly destroyed them.

Dean studied Rosie in the subdued tavern light. Had he, like his father, fallen for a woman inherently incapable of—or chronically unwilling to—conduct a relationship in a positive, open, constructive manner?

His mood threatened to tumble further, but he pulled it up with firm resolve, setting aside his own interests. Rosie didn't want him; that was clear. Badgering her would not help matters. No matter what, his child would be raised amid respect and courtesy, with two parents who worked together to create a stable environment. A loving environment…even if they didn't love each other.

Maybe if he backed off, she'd open up. Smile more. Knock a hole or two in the wall she'd erected around herself.

Rising, Dean started toward her, promising himself that his only agenda from now on was to establish a calm cordiality between them and to formulate a sane plan for cooperatively raising the child they'd created.

Rosemary looked around Tavern on the Highway, trying to ascertain whether Dean was already there. She turned her head in choppy motions, like a bird feeling vulnerable in an open field.

After spending the rest of her workday utterly distracted by thoughts that had nothing to do with work, she had come to a firm conclusion.

Well, pretty firm….

Sort of firm....

Not really firm at all. But she believed she was making the least crummy decision she could in a really difficult situation. The thought of sharing that decision with Dean was making her a nervous wreck, however, and she wanted to get it over with quickly.

"Rosemary."

The deep voice cut smoothly through the music and talking.

Dean wore a handsome sweater in cowboy tan, an attractive complement to his blue eyes and nut-brown hair. His shoulders appeared broader out of the white lab coat, and he looked relaxed and very, very...hot.

Rosie felt a dizzying sense of déjà vu, almost as if they were about to reenact the night they'd met. Except that he'd just called her Rosemary—instead of *Rosie*—for the first time.

"I've got a table away from the noise," he said, reaching automatically to put a guiding hand beneath her elbow. Before he connected with her, however, he stopped himself, letting his hand drop back to his side.

Nodding, she followed him, aware of the feminine smiles and lingering glances of appreciation he drew along the way.

When they reached the table, she plopped her large shoulder bag onto one of the four available chairs. As she sat, she noted the drinks waiting for them.

"I ordered for us," he acknowledged. "If you'd like something else, I'll head back to the bar."

Recalling the drinks he'd sent to the table the night they'd met, she frowned. "Is it a mixed drink? I'm not having any alcohol."

"It's orange juice."

She looked at the two tall tumblers. "Which one?"

"Both."

She looked up, remembering that he was a connoisseur of Pacific Northwest microbrews. "Orange juice over beer?"

He shrugged. "You can't drink. I'm fine with orange juice."

"That's nice of you." Her ex wouldn't have put himself out that way. Dean sat down, and Rosemary cleared her throat, wondering how to begin.

"Are you hungry?" Dean asked, drawing her attention to the Tavern's minibuffet.

"I'm ravenous at night, but…I'm a little nervous right now. I'd like to talk first."

His brows rose, but quickly fell again, his expression a handsome mask that hid his thoughts. He was different tonight, more subdued and…neutral. No hunger in his eyes, no humor lurking at the edges of his mouth. Rosemary told herself that a dispassionate Dean would be far easier to approach regarding the topic at hand.

She coughed lightly to clear her throat.

Then sighed.

Then she reached for her orange juice, took a shaky sip and replaced the glass on its cocktail napkin.

She folded her hands in her lap.

One of her feet began to tap madly, so she crossed her legs to quell the anxious motion.

Spit it out, Rosemary!

"I've been thinking about our situation all afternoon. It's hard to think of anything else, isn't it? I told one of my friends—she was here the night I met you—Daphne. I don't know whether you remember?"

"The blonde." Dean nodded. "My friend Len was smitten."

"Oh. Well, I told Daphne what was going on. I hope you don't mind—"

He waved the concern away. "I'd expect you to discuss a

major life event with your friends. I'd be more worried if you didn't. I assume you've told your family, too?"

She shifted uncomfortably. "No. I'd rather not tell my family until we have certain decisions ironed out."

Crossing his arms, Dean settled himself against the ladder-back chair, observing her soberly. He wasn't a husky man, but he was tall and broad-shouldered. He looked too big for the stingy piece of furniture. "Maybe," he said, "your family can help you reach those decisions."

She nearly groaned. If only he could appreciate the irony.

Her mother, after lamenting Rosemary's apparent inability to navigate birth control at the age of thirty-two, would remind her that the decision to forfeit one's independence this way lasted at least eighteen years.

One thing Rosemary had to say about Dean: at no time had he chosen the easy way out of this situation. He could have walked; she'd certainly given him the opportunity to turn a blind eye to her pregnancy.

Frowning, she folded the edges of her cocktail napkin. "We've both had a few days to let this sink in," she began, needing to know more about him before she said what she'd come here to say. "Have you—at any time—considered asking me to end the pregnancy?"

It took her a few seconds to lift her gaze from the napkin and let it focus on his face. She saw an expression she had not witnessed on him before. Blue lasers, his eyes pinned her with a steely intensity. His shoulders grew rigid, and he looked as if only a mighty effort allowed him to control his voice when he responded. "If you don't want this baby, I do. Your body is the one that has to go through nine months of pregnancy, I realize that, but you're carrying something that belongs to me, too. If you need help—with money, time, anything—I'll give it to you, but don't do anything—"

Rosemary held up a hand. "I'm not, I'm not." She shook

her head. "I asked because I wondered how committed you are to the idea of being a father." She smiled wryly. "I guess we're clear on that now."

He watched her closely a moment longer. Slowly, his shoulders began to relax.

What an interesting man he was. Never married although he was thirty-five, not above a one-night stand, yet willing to become a single father if necessary.

"Have you always wanted children?" she asked. "Or is this a philosophical conviction?"

He gave the question the consideration it was due. "I used to want children. In my twenties, I figured I'd be a father by the time I was thirty. Somewhere along the line I became less convinced, and more recently..." he hesitated "...I thought I'd marry, but wasn't sure kids were in the picture."

"That would have been all right with you?"

Again Dean gazed at her a long time before answering. "No. For a while I thought it would be, but...no." Uncrossing his arms, he leaned forward, moving his untouched orange juice to the side and resting his elbows on the table. "What about you? How eager are you to be a mother?"

That's what Daphne had asked her, and after getting off the phone with her longtime friend she'd spent the rest of last night letting the reality sink in. For as long as she could remember, she'd wanted the trappings of family life—dinners around a big table with everyone talking too much; holidays filled with chaos; summers that were lazy and laughter-filled. Neil, her ex, had convinced her that wanting to do family activities and needing to expand the family in order to do them were two entirely different things. They were already a family, just the two of them, he'd insisted, and someday they could seriously discuss the addition of children, when they were *both* ready.

Neil had decided he was ready to add a mistress before he became ready to add children, and even now, two years beyond the discovery, his betrayal still felt like a bayonet slashing at Rosemary's soul. That seemed so melodramatic, but it was true. She wished she could get over it, forget him, forget how good they had once felt. But she had pictured herself at eighty, with children and grandchildren and great-grandchildren… and with Neil, happily counting the wrinkles and the years. She had defied her family's warnings, braved their wagging heads and ignored how often the word *naive* came up in conversation so she could continue to believe in her dream.

Neil had taken much more than himself out of her life. Never before had she believed hope was something that could die; now she knew it was possible. To lose her dream, something so intrinsic to her spirit, was a feeling she never wanted to experience again.

She looked at Dean, waiting patiently for her answer. Was she eager to be a mother?

Last night, she had pictured her future with—and without—a child. She'd imagined being a single mother, in a small town and in a city…perhaps Portland, but perhaps someplace entirely new, where she would be a stranger among strangers. She'd bathed herself in the details and the feelings that had come up, trying not to judge or censor her reactions, and finally she'd found her way to what was, for her, the truth.

Being a single parent, like her mother before her, was not her dream come true. But having a child to hold, to love unconditionally, to introduce to butterflies and rainbows and monster slides and swimming pools, to wipe sticky hands and dry salty tears, and to know that until the end of her own life, she would love someone with every breath she took—

"Yes," she said aloud and without any doubt. "I'm eager to be a mother. I'm excited about the baby." It felt *soooo* good to be able to say it out loud! Hopefully when the time came, she would be able to say the same thing to her family—without stuttering or apologizing for being the sole Jeffers woman who wanted the whole package—mother, father, backseat full of kids. "I don't think it's too soon to start addressing the baby's needs."

Dean shifted, sitting up straighter. He had begun to smile when she said she was thrilled. Once she mentioned the baby's needs, however, he came to full attention, serious as a judge. "I plan to be financially responsible throughout my child's life. If there's anything you need right now—"

"Oh, no, no! I wasn't talking about finances. I don't need money. And neither does the baby right now."

"There are things you'll need. And days you might not feel up to working. I'll see my lawyer and set something up."

"That is not necessary, really." He started to rebut, but she held firm. "If there are things you want to buy for the baby, that's up to you, but *I* do not want financial help, especially not before she's born. Thank you, anyway." She smiled to sweeten the edict, but was careful not to appear to waver, because Dean Kingsley could be stubborn.

He took her words in, not liking them much, though he nodded his acceptance. He raised a brow. "'She,' huh?"

"Or he."

"When it's time to pick out names, do you mind if I help? At least with the middle name."

Baby names. Rosemary blinked in surprise. He wanted to pick out baby names? She nearly laughed aloud at the irony.

Years ago, when she and Neil had still been in college, they'd gone to Canon Beach for the weekend. Two darling chubby toddler girls in tiny bikinis had played in the sand next to them, and Rosemary had asked Neil what he might like to name a little girl if they ever had one. He'd leaped from their blanket as if the sand had caught fire, ran into the ocean and returned twenty minutes later, dripping wet and silent.

Back in Portland, Rosemary had relayed the story to Vi, who told her that playing "What Do We Name the Baby?"

with a man was like "handing him a knife and inviting him to cut off his own testicles." Rosemary had not broached the topic again until they'd been married three years.

Now she managed a wry smile. "As long as your favorite names are pronounceable and have nothing to do with states, cars or local tributaries, I think we can work it out."

For the first time this evening, she got a glimpse of the more relaxed Dean, the one who laughed easily. "Aww. I was hoping for Montana if it's a girl and Nissan if it's a boy. I guess I can bend."

"Montana is kind of pretty, actually."

They shared their first un-tense moment since the night they'd met. Rosemary hated to ruin it by introducing another issue, but she'd come here with an agenda that had to be addressed.

"What?" he said when she hesitated. "You're frowning again. Whatever it is, why not get it over with fast, like pulling off a Band-Aid?"

"I usually use a wet towel and soak a Band-Aid off."

"Sounds time-consuming."

She nodded.

"Gotcha." He reached for his orange juice and settled back. "Okay, take your time."

She took a deep breath. No matter how much time she took, this was still going to be awkward in the extreme. Her heart thumped heavily. If only she knew more about him….

"All right," she breathed, gripping the table's edge as if she were hanging from a cliff. "You asked me once if I was married before. I was. My plan was never to be married again. When I moved to Honeyford, I wanted to focus on my career and the community. I like it here. A lot."

From her first word, Dean gave her his full attention, as usual. His face was a mask of polite interest, using neutrality to invite her to keep speaking.

"Being a single mother will change how I feel about the town," she continued, "and how the town feels about me. I've had half a dozen people describe the scandal of the interim librarian." At his puzzled expression, Rosemary explained, "She had a pierced lip and tried to introduce the book club to erotica."

Dean's mouth twitched.

"I've given a lot of thought to moving away." She saw Dean tense perceptibly, so she stated quickly, "I've decided that I want to stay." Like magic, his shoulders relaxed again. "At least for now," she added cautiously. "But being the single pregnant librarian doesn't sound like a good idea, especially when people discover that you're the father."

Placing his glass on the table, Dean shrugged. "Why? I don't like to brag, but most people in town find me pretty likeable."

Rosemary looked at the thick, earth-brown hair he kept neatly trimmed, at the features that were classically handsome and aging like fine wine, at the blue eyes that smiled even when his lips hadn't moved a bit, and she knew that although he was being facetious, he had told the truth. Women probably faked all manner of ailments merely to visit the pharmacist for advice.

"It's going to seem ridiculous that a librarian and a pharmacist didn't have the sense to use birth control, don't you think?" she said.

Dean's eyes darkened. "Obviously 'sense' is not my forte when you're in my arms." He paused. "Past tense, I mean."

The temperature in the tavern—or simply inside Rosemary—shot up ten degrees. *Concentrate on the topic.* A gentle, ironic smile curved his lips, and suddenly she remembered exactly how they felt pressed to hers…and to other parts of her body. *Concentrate.*

"Anyway, I think there would be a lot of gossip. And even

if it isn't ill intentioned, it would be difficult to deal with. Difficult for the library and, when the baby grows up enough to understand, difficult for her. Or him."

A silence as pregnant as Rosemary ensued. Dean broke it.

"What's your solution?"

Her heart began to race at a dizzying speed. "I think it's not unreasonable to cater to the conservatives in this case. I mean, I think sometimes discretion is the better part of valor."

He raised a brow. "Yeah?"

As gentlemanly as he was, he didn't intend to rescue her. Rosemary broke a sweat.

"Yes. So here's what I propose." She winced when the last word left her mouth. Couldn't help it. Deep breath. "I think we should…or at least *I* would like to…for the baby's sake more than anything…get…" *Say it, Rosemary, say it.* "Mm… Mmm…" She swallowed, licked her dry lips. "Mmm-a…" Oh, God in heaven.

She was going to have a heart attack before she said the damn word. Maybe there was another solution, after all. Maybe she really should move….

Dean reached into his back pocket and withdrew a leather wallet. He pulled out a few bills, tossed them onto the table and reached for her wrist. "Let's go."

Chapter Eight

They wound up driving their own vehicles to Dean's apartment. He led the way, driving slowly enough for her to follow even though she knew exactly how to get there. Upon arriving on Main Street, Dean directed her around the rear of his building, where they parked and walked up the alley entrance to his place.

Neither of them mentioned her botched proposal again until they were seated at the small dining table, eating omelets he'd made expertly with Gruyère cheese, oil-cured olives and thin crescent-shaped slices of avocado.

"You're good at this," Rosemary commented, awkwardly breaking their tense silence. "I'm not a very inspired cook."

"I took a class when I was in college. My roommate and I thought it would be a good way to meet girls."

"Was it?"

"For him. He married someone he met the first night."

"And she got a husband who could cook."

"No. He dropped the class."

"You stayed and learned how to make omelets?"

"And fish tacos and a dangerous chocolate cake." He pointed the tines of his fork in her direction. "*You're* getting a husband who can cook."

With the point of their meeting on the table, they both set down their forks.

Wiping his mouth, Dean rested his forearms on the table and made his usual straightforward eye contact. "I like the idea of getting married."

Rosemary nodded slowly. With that one decision agreed upon, a host of new issues opened up, and her stomach roiled. "It seems like the best solution…for now."

Dean watched her closely. "Are you putting a time limit on it?"

He'd hit fine-point number one solidly on the head. "Yes. I think it should be time-limited from the outset. Everything should be as clear and businesslike as possible to avoid confusion and resentment down the line." She'd already given this point extensive consideration and was able to present her case without stumbling. "Confusion and resentment on the parents' part is toxic for a child. If we plan in advance exactly when and how we're going to separate, then when the time comes we should be able to do it amicably. And that will be good for everyone."

"What makes you certain there'll be a time when we want to part?"

The question truly shocked her. "We don't know each other. We're getting married for the sake of the baby…and maybe our jobs. But mostly for the baby."

"Marriages have begun on flimsier foundations than wanting to create a family for a child."

"I doubt those marriages last."

"I'm sure they take work." He buttered one of the rolls he'd set out. "Then again, all marriages do. We'd be more aware of that than most, which could give us a leg up."

She frowned, watching the steady, even swipes of the butter knife over the bread. "I've already told you, I don't want to be married again. Ever."

"Which seems to be the real crux of the matter." Calmly, he took a bite of the roll then reached for his fork and tucked into the omelet again.

Suddenly they could have been discussing Honeyford's plan to hold a spring parade rather than a matter that would affect the rest of their lives; he was that nonchalant. The tide of tension inside Rosemary rose dangerously. "How can you still be hungry when we're talking about this?"

"About marriage?" He shrugged as he forked up another bite of egg oozing with melted cheese. "See, that's the difference between us. The thought of marriage doesn't kill my appetite."

I have good reason, she almost said, but wisely remained silent. They didn't have to know everything about each other to make this work. *For the length of time that it had to work.*

"All right." Someone had to be reasonable and realistic here, and obviously it was going to be her. "What I'm thinking is that a year and a half of marriage will give us time to have the baby, establish that you are the legal father and that we tried to make the relationship a go. Unfortunately, because we rushed into things, we will realize that we need to separate before the baby is old enough to be confused and hurt by our continual problems. We'll say we did our best, but the writing was on the wall."

"Why didn't we get counseling?"

"Because—" She shook her head and blinked. "What?"

"Counseling. Professional advice about how to make it work."

Rosemary squinted as if that might help her see his point. "We're not trying to make it work."

He washed the food down with decaf then nodded. "Ah, right. What if someone asks that, though? It's a reasonable question, especially with a child involved."

"We'll say we tried, and *it didn't help*."

He gazed at her. "Pity. So a year and a half. Is there a contingency plan if we decide we don't want to separate?"

"We're not going to decide that."

"*You* might. I'm incredibly easy to live with." Polishing off his roll, he spied the one she hadn't yet touched and plucked it off her plate. She regarded him dubiously as he picked up his knife to split and butter *her* bread.

"Why do you want to talk about staying together?" she asked, snatching the roll back. "If you want a wife that badly, why haven't you gotten married before now?" She took a big bite of roll. She was the pregnant one, after all, the one who needed the most nourishment. If he could eat during this conversation, then by golly so would she.

He looked at his plate, and she wondered if he was going to respond at all. Finally, instead of answering her, he looked up and asked a question. "Why did you go to the motel with me?"

Oh, Lord in heaven, what a question. "Lust," she said baldly, shoving every other memory from her mind. "I was using you. Sorry, but that's all."

He laughed. "That statement doesn't carry the same negativity for a man that it does for a woman. We're generally happy to have you go ahead and use us. From whom were you on the rebound?"

"I didn't say I was on the rebound."

Dean narrowed his eyes.

Fine. "My ex, of course." She took another bite of the roll, this time a big one. "Good bread."

"It's from Honey Bea's. I'll take you there one morning before work for decaf coffee and the best apple fritters you've ever tasted."

"One apple fritter has enough calories to feed a major city," she informed him, seriously tucking into the omelet now while simultaneously shaking her head. "Do they serve dry toast?"

"I sincerely hope not. Why are you worried about calories? Your body's great."

"I've always been kind of fleshy. By month nine of this pregnancy I'll probably weigh more than you."

"Fleshy." This time he muttered an expletive. "Women and body image. This is why I won't carry weight-loss aids in the pharmacy." He buttered the other half of her roll. "So you were on the rebound from your ex-husband. Somehow I was under the impression you've been divorced awhile."

"Two years." She held out her hand. He put the roll into it.

"And you're still rebounding?"

"Not 'still.'" She put a little bit of the omelet onto the roll. "You were my first rebound. And my last. I'm done with all that. I'm going to be celibate now." She popped the impromptu sandwich into her mouth and rolled her eyes in pleasure. "I can't believe how hungry I get at night."

"Join the club."

Rosemary glanced up from the food to find him gazing at her with an appetite that couldn't be misunderstood. Her body responded like a firecracker set alight.

Exploding low in her body, desire rushed through her, making her limbs go weak as noodles. The food lost its appeal.

Dean leaned forward, almost imperceptibly, but his intention was clear in every angle of his tightly wound body. He looked as if he was waiting for her to give him the okay so he could leap across the table to devour her instead of the food.

Wanting him wasn't the question. Whether Rosemary was willing to give in to the urges trying to overtake her—that was the question.

Never one to be carried away by the needs of her body, she could hardly fathom the strength of her desire to rip off his clothes and to feel him again over, inside and around her.

"A year and a half." His voice, deep and gravelly, interrupted her thoughts. "That won't be nearly enough time to burn out this desire. If we make love again, even once, I'll end up wanting you more, not less. So my answer to 'Do you want to get married?' Yes." His mouth quirked. "Great idea. But unless we're going to keep it open-ended—and very real—I think we should call it a night tonight."

Even though he'd made a statement, a question lingered in his tone and in his eyes.

An open-ended marriage...one that was 'real'...

What made a marriage real? Sex? That wasn't enough to turn a legal union for the baby's sake into the genuine article—or to make a marriage last. Sometimes not even the best intentions or the strongest desire could do that.

Edging out sexual hunger came the fear that was never far from the surface for Rosemary. What if she really did fall for Dean? Or for the dream of a traditional family again? What if she bought it all, hook, line and sinker, and he turned out to be another really good salesman?

Her sister Lucy was a family law attorney in Portland, specializing in divorce for women. Lucy had handled the dissolution of Rosemary's first marriage, and Rosemary planned to have her handle this one, too. Lucy was a pit bull, one of the most sought-after attorneys in Oregon. She didn't have a sentimental or romantic bone in her entire body.

Lucy was thirty-four, but she had never thrown herself into

a relationship with the fervor of an Olympic athlete going for the gold. She had never cried for months because a man no longer loved her.

Channel Lucy.

As it turned out, Rosemary didn't have to say a word. Dean read her answer on her face.

"A shame," he murmured, removing the napkin from his lap and setting it on the table.

The evening was over.

She thought—although she wasn't positive—that they had just come to an agreement: a time-limited marriage, no sex.

That was good. That was…that was smart.

The next time she and Dean were together they would need to discuss an actual prenuptial agreement—printed on paper with a watermark, witnessed signatures, the whole nine yards. Lucy would scream if Rosemary entered another marriage without one.

And, her sister would positively murder her if she knew that right now Rosemary wasn't thinking about practicalities at all, but rather imagining what it would feel like to have one more night of astounding sex with Dean then walk to the bakery in the morning before work, thinking of nothing more important than the calories in an apple fritter…and of how fortunate a woman was when her lover thought she was simply delicious just the way she was.

Three days later, Dean had agreed to allow Lucy Jeffers to draft a prenuptial agreement. It would include the details of the apparently inevitable dissolution of his marriage to Rosemary and specify that he agreed to an uncontested divorce when the time came.

"Give me something to do," he told his brother as they stood before a section of barbed-wire fencing Fletcher was working on. It was Sunday, the day Dean typically spent riding his mountain bike when the weather was good, or working on plans for the clinic he dreamed of opening. More recently, he spent his day off here at Pine Road Ranch, playing uncle to his brother's new family and enjoying one of his sister-in-law's stellar home-cooked meals. Today, though, he was here to get advice—from the brother he'd once thought wasn't fit to advise a toddler not to play in the street.

"What are you doing," he pressed when Fletcher continued to work without responding, "twisting those pieces together? Do you have another pair of pliers?"

Fletcher continued to work steadily and with practiced skill. "This is manual labor, Deano. I don't want you to hurt yourself. Why don't you stand there, look pretty and keep talking. So far, this has been the most interesting conversation we've ever had."

"Hand me the damn pliers." Shrugging, Fletcher complied, and Dean attacked the fence, working without skill, but with a fervor fueled by frustration.

Fletcher stepped back and took a long drink of the lemonade Claire had packed for him. Then he sat on the hard ground and recapped what his brother had told him. "So you're going to get married in time to fulfill that one condition of Victor's will, but you're not going to *stay* married long enough to actually claim your inheritance. And this woman, Rosemary, doesn't know you need to be married two years to inherit the building on Main, because you haven't told her about the will at all, even though this isn't a love match to begin with. Have I got that right?"

"That's the gist of it." Dean gave a vicious twist of the pliers.

"Don't snap that wire. If you leave me with more work to do, it'll piss me off, and I've been working damn hard lately to control my temper."

Dean clenched his jaw as he wrapped one piece of wire

around another. "I thought marriage has mellowed you naturally."

"It has. Toward Claire and the kids. Fools still try my patience."

Looking over his shoulder, Dean glared. "Meaning I'm a fool."

Fletcher removed his sweat-stained Stetson and scratched his scalp. "Ah, let's see, how did Claire tell me to word this crap? Oh, yeah. I don't agree with your *decisions* in this *arena,* Dean. I'm afraid you may get yourself into some trouble." He replaced his hat and spit on the ground. "But as soon as you take your head out of your ass you'll be fine."

Dean tossed the pliers into Fletcher's tool kit. "Just say it."

"All right. From what you've told us, Rosemary wouldn't go on a date with you, much less get married, unless she felt she had no choice. So you've got nothing to lose by telling her about Victor's asinine will. Tell her the Kingsleys put the *fun* in *dysfunction* and that you can't inherit the building you live and work in unless you get married by summer and stay married two years. That's only a half year longer than she already wants. No big deal." He reached into a canvas lunch box and withdrew a thick cookie that looked as if it had been made for a giant. Taking a huge bite of his wife's baking, Fletcher grinned. "She knows what I like." He chewed contentedly, and Dean wanted to kill him.

"The thing is," Fletcher continued once he'd swallowed, "you don't want to tell Rosemary the truth even though you had no problem telling Amanda. Seems to me that's because Amanda was the woman you always thought you'd marry— cool, intellectual, didn't give a rat's ass whether you were marrying for love or not. Very safe for you since you don't like to feel anything below the neck."

"Hey, that's bull—"

Fletcher held up a finger—not the index one. "You asked. I respect you too much to sugarcoat the horrible truth."

Dean clenched his fists to keep from picking up the pliers and hitting his brother in the head with them. "And the horrible truth is?"

"Loving a woman is the most ass-kicking, out-of-control, cannot-get-your-head-around-it, frightening feeling in the world." He leveled Dean with a laser-sharp stare. "I'm talking about real love."

"As opposed to?"

"Everything else. The stuff people fill their time with so they won't be alone or be able to think too much. Being with someone because you want a relationship isn't remotely the same as being with a woman because you can't imagine taking another breath without her in your life."

Dean shook his head. "I feel as if I'm having an out-of-body experience, listening to *you* give a dissertation on love."

It was a fact that before he'd met his wife Fletcher had spent his life disdaining affection. He took no offense.

"Thing is," he said, "people assume love is a soft feeling. It hasn't been for me, and I doubt it will be for you. When you need a woman like you need air and water, you'll be on fire until you know she wants you, too. Then you'll stay on fire, wanting to keep her happy, figuring out how to let her know she's the best thing that ever happened to you. Add kids to the mix, and every muscle in your body will be on alert, ready to kill or die for them. It's damned exhausting."

"But you love it."

"Wouldn't have it any other way. Ever. That's what's so freaking terrifying. Once you meet *the* woman, you know damn well that if anything ever happened to her, you'd want to die, too." His gaze narrowed. "When I met Claire, she made me want things I thought I'd given up half a lifetime ago. So how is it for you? You haven't known Rosemary that long."

Dean pulled a hand down his face and took a deep breath. Everything his brother said whomped him smack in the gut. He'd started to feel that way about Rosemary the first night. "I've known her long enough."

Fletcher nodded slowly. "And you don't want to tell her that you need to get married on account of your crazy father's will, because…"

"It'll louse up any chance to make her believe I'm falling in love with her." Dean's mouth was dry as old hay. He couldn't swallow with guilt choking him. "I'm right not to tell her… right?"

Fletcher tossed his big bro a pitying glance. "No, you're out of your mind. She's going to draw up that prenup, and if the marriage only lasts eighteen months, you're screwed. Six more and at least you'll walk away with your business."

"Well, what the hell?" Uncharacteristically, Dean burst into anger. "Now you're saying the inheritance is more important than love?"

"No. But according to the will, the building on Main goes to the city if you default. Doug Thorpe sits on the city council. He's been yammering to everyone who'll listen that a new upscale restaurant downtown will draw tourist dollars. I think the pharmacy itself is safe, but he'd love to get his hands on a couple of the storefronts next door, so there goes your clinic. And, you'll have to start paying rent on the drugstore. With a child to raise, that's going to be a burden. You don't want to have to start working longer hours when you've got a baby. You gain nothing by losing the building."

Frustration turned Dean's limbs stiff yet quivering like plucked strings. "The worst part of this, the absolute worst part, is lying to her. And being terrified that if I tell her the truth I'll lose her and the baby." He eyed his brother. "There better be a solution on the tip of your tongue. You came out of this will debacle smelling like a rose. Give me some coaching here."

Fletcher's features melted into the grateful serenity that the mention of his family never failed to evoke. "Sometimes, Deano, I think that the fact things worked out with Claire was dumb luck." His voice turned into the kinder rumble Dean was still getting used to. "That or divine pity. But Claire was a widow with one good marriage under her belt already. She was a wife and mother through and through. From what you've told us about Rosemary—and you don't seem to know *that* much about her—marriage was the furthest thing from her mind the night you two hooked up. Seems to me that not telling her about the will is playing with fire."

Pressing fingers to his forehead, Dean scrubbed at his brow. He was caught in a damned tangled web. He didn't know whether to blame his father for adding the marriage codicil to his will...or himself, for falling in love when he'd least expected to.

Chapter Nine

"Make him sign in front of a notary. Don't let him off the hook for any reason. But, if his lawyer quibbles over any-thing—*anything*—in that prenup, then I don't want you getting within fifty feet of the thing with a pen."

Lucy Jeffers's voice sounded like rubber bands snapping as it came through the cell phone. Tucked beneath Rosemary's arm was the prenuptial agreement Lucy had overnighted, and Rosemary held an umbrella over her head to protect the large envelope from the steady rain as she made her way up Main Street to King's Pharmacy.

"Honest to God, Rosemary—" the strain in Lucy's voice was palpable "—I don't know why in heaven you think you need to marry this dude. Women have babies on their own all the time, not that I think *that's* a brilliant idea. But it'd be a helluva lot easier to be stuck with a kid and a nanny instead of a kid and some jerk—"

"Dean's not a jerk. He's not like that," Rosemary muttered,

acutely aware that a) She and her sister had already had this conversation, b) Lucy was never going to be soothed when it came to a man, marriage and one of her family members, and c) She was walking down a public street and did not want to talk about this. "Dean's actually very reasonable—" she began sotto voce, but Lucy cut her off so loudly Rosemary pulled the phone away from her ear.

"Don't!" The severe admonishment echoed like a tuning fork. "Do not romanticize him. Rosemary, promise me you'll save your..." Lucy searched for the right word. "...fairy-tale fantasies for your journal and *this time* apply your brains to the real world."

Rosemary winced. By the time she pressed End Call, she felt as if she'd run several miles in sand. All she wanted was a nap. And a good cry.

"She's trying to protect you. She doesn't want to see you get hurt again. No one does," their sister Evelyn had said when Rosemary phoned last night to tell her about the baby, the decision she'd made and Lucy's help with the prenuptial agreement. *"This is why she's a top lawyer. I only wish you were better at protecting yourself, honey. Have you told Mom?"*

Rosemary hadn't, not yet. She had a one-person-a-day threshold when it came to disappointing family members.

Morning sickness encroached on her previously nausea-free day. She wasn't certain this time whether it was physical or emotional. Loneliness, bone deep and chilling, assailed her.

Clutching the handle of the umbrella in a death grip, she put her free hand over her stomach. *Don't you worry,* she told it telepathically, comforting the tiny, tiny life inside her as if it, too, were concerned about isolation, *we're going to be fine, just fine, the two of us. And you'll have your...* Her breath caught just a little. *Your daddy. I think he's going to be very hands-on.*

It was true. She wasn't worried about Dean's involvement with their child. He'd been accepting of and excited about the baby from the start.

She frowned and caught the toe of her pump on an uneven piece of sidewalk. Not once in any of their conversations had Lucy or Evelyn mentioned their future niece or nephew, even though Rosemary's child would be the first baby in the family.

Suddenly, her footsteps, which had been dragging, picked up the pace as she advanced on King's Pharmacy. She would get this over with then phone Daphne for a reassuring pick-me-up. Marriage and babies were always positives for her.

Reminding herself of Lucy's admonition to be businesslike and unemotional when dealing with the prenup, Rosemary closed her umbrella, shook out the water and swung open the pharmacy door. Amid the tinkling of the bells, she walked briskly into the store. At this time of morning, the pharmacy would be open, which meant Dean would be in the back, filling prescriptions and doling out advice.

Heels clicking along the linoleum, she looked neither left nor right, hoping as she always did when she entered the pharmacy that she wouldn't run into anyone she knew.

Gonna have to get over that one, she thought, *if you're going to be married to the pharmacist…married for a while, anyway.*

Immediately when she walked in, the inherent friendliness and charm of the place struck her. The store could be divided into three distinct parts: the dry-goods aisles occupying the center of the shop; an old-fashioned soda fountain, which was past the dry goods to her left; and the pharmacy, tucked all the way in the back. Displays of candy and small gift items greeted her on the way in, but Dean spared his customers the usual commercial assault. Here, the candy was locally made and attractively packaged. Ditto on the gifts. Rosemary got the feeling Dean was selling Honeyford as much as anything else. *Welcome locals. Welcome tourists,* this store seemed to say. *I hope you like it here as much as I do.*

Unexpectedly, Rosemary felt as if she were on the verge of tears. "Hormones," she muttered under her breath and decided to get this done quickly so she could head to the library and keep herself busy.

"Rosemary!" Her name, sweetly accented with a Southern drawl, drew Rosemary's attention. "The boys and I were just talking about coming to story hour this afternoon."

After an initial clutch of apprehension, Rosemary glanced left to see a woman who was a frequent patron of the library. The young woman had a daughter still in diapers and two young sons who seemed to love the library as much as their mother did.

"Hello, Claire," she greeted, pleased that she was remembering the first names of most of the people who came to story hour at the library. "I almost didn't recognize you without Rosalind on your hip."

Claire rolled her eyes. "I know. My husband says I need to stop wearing her in the sling all the time. She's fifteen months, and she'd still rather ride than walk." Claire's joyful laugh further relaxed Rosemary. "I love carrying them, though. That time of their lives doesn't last long enough for me."

A strong yearning assailed Rosemary. How wonderful it would be to sit down with a mother and discuss everything baby—strollers and slings, diapers (cloth or disposable?), first smiles and first foods and the best methods for helping them sleep through the night. When should she and Dean announce that they were going to have a baby? When were they going to get married? There were still so many details to iron out.

Eager suddenly to see Dean, she politely excused herself. "It was good to run into you, Claire." She tilted her head in the direction of the pharmacy. "I need to see...the, um, pharmacist, so—"

"Dean's at the soda fountain." Claire reached for Rosemary's arm—somewhat eagerly, Rosemary thought. "Come on."

Young voices rang out as they approached that end of the store.

"How'm I doin', Uncle Dean? How'm I doin'?"

"Outstanding, buddy. Good job eating all the malt balls that fall."

"I don't want to waste 'em."

Claire's younger son, Orlando, stood behind the soda fountain as he ladled candy atop a dish of ice cream. His older brother, Will, very carefully spooned thick hot fudge over a sundae already gilded with toppings. And supervising it all was the man she had come to see, handsome as sin in his white pharmacist's coat, holding Claire's youngest child, the toddler Rosalind, as she experimented with putting chocolate fingerprints on the cheek of the man cuddling her.

It all looked so...right.

I wonder if this is what an out-of-body experience is like? Rosemary wondered, feeling as if she were floating.

"Hey!" Laughing, Dean reached up to capture the sticky fingers painting his cheek. Holding the tiny hand, he pretended to be horrified by the chocolate smears, but then stuck out the tip of his tongue and gave one short finger a swipe.

The boys *eeewwed,* Rosalind squealed, and, beside Rosemary, Claire laughed softly. "He's great with them."

Uncle. Belatedly, Rosemary realized what Orlando had called Dean. Her jaw dropped enough for her open mouth to accommodate a waffle cone. Of course, people used *Uncle* simply as a term of affection all the time, so it could be that—

"I was a widow when I met Fletcher," Claire confided in

a quiet voice. "I thought my boys would grow up without a man around and that having a mama would have to be enough. Now they've got two wonderful men—their daddy and their Uncle Dean." She looked at Rosemary, her eyes aglow if a bit tentative, and her voice soft. "He's going to be a terrific father someday."

She knows. The realization hit Claire like lightening on a hay bale.

"You and Dean are..." she pointed toward him, her brain moving like sludge through a sewer "...related by marriage?"

"Yep. Dean is my husband's brother. I met him, though, before I met Fletcher, which was a good thing, because Fletcher made me wonder whether Kingsley men were fit to be around little ones." Once again, her gay laughter put Rosemary at ease...almost.

"What's, um, *wrong* with Fletcher?"

"Oh, he just needed a good woman to smooth his rough edges." After a brief pause, Claire grinned beautifully. "And I needed him to rough up some of my smooth ones."

She looked at Rosemary, and suddenly seemed unsure of whether she should speak again. Rosemary both dreaded and couldn't wait to hear what Claire was going to say next.

"Dean's the opposite of my husband in so many ways. They're like dark and white chocolate. Fletcher still keeps his distance with everyone except family. But Dean..." Claire smiled with sincere fondness. "He puts everyone at ease. He's got a heart for people that's as big as the sun. Fletcher says Dean's carrying half the town on his ledgers. If someone doesn't have insurance, he finds a way to make sure they get their prescriptions filled no matter what. People aren't afraid to come to him when they need something. He never makes you feel foolish or small for asking." Appearing slightly apologetic, Claire concluded, "That was probably more than

I should have said, but I think sometimes Honeyford takes Dean for granted because he's always been good."

Rosemary's gaze strayed from Claire—her future temporary sister-in-law if Dean signed the prenup—to the man who, Rosemary knew, had not "*always* been good." In fact, the night they'd first met, he'd been quite, quite bad.

A disturbing thought—the kind of thought that sounded exactly like her mother's voice—made her breath catch. Maybe Dean did that kind of thing—seduced women in out-of-the-way bars and motels—more than anyone knew. *May*be he was like a politician, smooth as butter when people were looking, but with a secret life that could curl a horse's mane. Maybe he—

"Hey, give me that spoon, you little monkey." Rosemary emerged from her blind panic to see Dean laughing as he tried to pry a spoon from the resistant Rosalind's tiny hand. "Soon as you're steady on your feet, Uncle Dean is going to teach you how to play T-ball." He glanced up and grinned as Claire approached the marble-topped counter. "This one's got quite a grip—" For the first time, he noticed Rosemary, still standing several feet away. His words stopped, and his gaze lingered.

"What did you give her?" Claire asked, nodding to the spoon.

"White Chocolate Peppermint Patty," he responded, his attention still on Rosemary. "I needed her expert opinion. Hello."

Rosemary wasn't certain whether he mouthed the greeting to her or murmured it. Either way, the intimacy made her toes curl.

Claire reached across the counter to take the spoon from her daughter and laughed when Rosalind protested. "If that's a new flavor, I'd say it's a winner. Here, let me wipe her mouth."

Returning his attention to his sister-in-law, Dean came around the counter to transfer his wriggling niece to her mother's arms. Then he turned to Rosemary.

Her body began to tingle. An ocean of sensation rose up from her toes until it roared in her ears. *It's nothing, nothing,* she told herself. *You are not your feelings. You are a sane, intelligent, levelheaded person—*

He smiled. Just for her.

Hic.

Her eyes widened as a painful hiccup jerked her body. *You are in charge of how you react to any given situa—*

Hic!

"Ow." She pressed a hand to her sternum.

"Ooh. Are you okay?" Claire looked at her, mild concern tinged with amusement.

"Yes, I—" *Hic.* "'Scuse me."

Dean reached a hand beneath her elbow. She tightened her arm against her side so as not to drop the prenup. His touch was gentle, his expression gorgeously disturbed by her discomfort. *Oh, God, a woman could get lost in that expression—*

Hic!

"Can you take a deep breath?" Dean modeled the breath he had in mind, making his chest rise and fall slowly.

"I'm fine. Really."

"Mom!" Orlando, Claire's younger son, called from behind the counter. "Uncle Deano! Look! I'm finished. Lookit how big it is!" He pointed a spoon dripping with strawberry sauce at a lopsided sundae. He'd covered the ice-cream mountain in candy. A landslide appeared imminent.

"Oh, dear," his mother said.

But Uncle Dean gave him the thumbs-up. "Good job, buddy. Any day you want to work here after school, you let me know."

The older boy, Will, whom Rosemary had always found very sweet, looked up from his more circumspect creation. "Me, too, Uncle Dean?"

"Of course. You'll be in charge of the daily audit. I'll rely on you to keep our food costs down." Will had no idea what his uncle meant, but the job sounded impressive, and he puffed up like a peacock as he smiled at his mother.

Family. Place. Permanence. That was the fourth part of King's Pharmacy, and it was almost as tangible right now as the dry goods, pharmacy or soda fountain.

Glancing back at Rosemary, Dean winked, handsome creases edging his grin. "Training the next generation of Kingsley soda jerks," he quipped. Then his gaze dropped, briefly and privately, to her stomach.

The tides of feeling surged again from Rosemary's toes and by the time they made it to her head, she was dizzy. *Oh, no...*

Hic...hic. Hic! Hic! Hic!

"If you drink apple juice backwards with your fingers in your ears, hiccups go away," Will advised sagely.

Dean glanced at Claire, who shrugged and whispered, "I made that up."

"Come on." He began to pull on Rosemary's elbow to guide her. "Hold down the fort, guys. Claire, if you need to head out before I get back, just leave everything." Guiding Rosemary, he said, "Let's get those taken care of."

With her thoughts buzzing like an active hive, Rosemary let herself be led up the stairs in the back of the store and into Dean's immaculate-as-before apartment. Once inside, she stood in her trench coat, body straight and tense, her stillness punctuated only by the intermittent bounce of the hiccups.

Closing the door, Dean came up behind her and tried to slip her purse off her shoulder. Startled, she grabbed the strap.

"Sorry. Why don't you put down everything you're carrying, and I'll help you get rid of those hiccups."

Embarrassed that she was so jumpy, Rosemary said, "I'm sure they'll go away soon. I almost never get hic—*hic!*—cups." Shifting the large envelope beneath her arm into her hands, she got down to business, hoping that would calm the jittery sensation in her body. "I brought the prenuptial agreement my sister drew up."

He hesitated before accepting the envelope. "You want a cup of coffee?"

"Now? No. I mean, you don't have to read it now…and I have to get to work."

"I wasn't going to read it now. I just thought you might like to relax a minute. And talk."

"Talk?" *Hic.*

"Yes, Rosie. Talk. That's when two people sit, sometimes opposite each other, sometimes side by side, and they converse about any topic that has meaning for them." He looked at the envelope, a frown between his brows. "In this case, our marriage might be a good conversation starter."

He closed his eyes briefly, brought his thumb and forefinger up and rubbed before looking at her again. "Sorry. Sarcasm is not my favorite mode of expression."

She smiled. Who said things like "mode of expression" in normal conversation these days? Every now and again Dean would pop out some comment or action that made him seem as if he came from another era. Like his store downstairs. She liked it. "You're not sarcastic. Usually."

"Really? I feel sarcastic lately."

The tilt to his lips and the wry, almost sad expression in his eyes gave the moment an intimacy that for a moment made Rosemary *feel* married to him.

Hic!

"Oh, for God's sake," he muttered. Tossing the envelope

onto a slim buffet table that stood against the back of the couch, he reached for her purse again without asking and tossed it onto the table, as well. "Give me your coat."

Don't wanna. Rosemary knew she should leave before her thoughts ran away with her, but she did have something—a little point she and Lucy had changed in the prenup—that she needed to mention to him.

"I'll only stay a minute," she assured him, unnecessarily as he didn't seem concerned about getting back to work quickly this morning. Untying the belt of her trench coat, she let him grab it in one hand and toss it, too, over the buffet.

"Come on." Taking her arm, he pulled her casually around the sofa, where he directed her to one of the leather cushions and seated himself beside her. "Turn," he said.

"What?" *Hic.*

Shaking his head—*I'm not doing this dance again, Rosie*—he turned her shoulders, forcing her either to shift the rest of her body or to twist herself into a yoga pose guaranteed to squoosh the teeny tiny baby.

Dean's hands settled onto her shoulders. She felt his palms through the thin material of the wrap dress she'd donned this morning. His touch was warm and heavy and grounding. *Hic. Oh, man. Hic, hic, hic.*

"I, um, I do have something…a little point…I need to discuss with—"

"Shh. We'll talk in a minute. Relax first." Sliding his hands down the outside of her arms, he lifted her shoulders until they were hunched around her ears, held them there a moment and then let them drop. Not at all a sexy move, which was rather reassuring, but definitely relaxing.

Stretching her shoulders back, he used his thumbs to work into the muscles, the massage rhythmic and efficient, and her body began to settle into his capable hands.

"Hiccups can be caused by tension in the diaphragmatic

muscle," he murmured, his mellow voice seeming like yet another aspect of the massage. "Once they begin, the muscle contraction takes on a life of its own." His fingers walked slowly down either side of her spine. Rosemary had been tense for so many weeks, she almost moaned. "Some people try to relax the muscle by distracting themselves."

"Like drinking apple juice upside down with their fingers in their ears." She remembered Will's suggestion.

Dean chuckled softly. "I'd never heard that one before. But yes, like that." He used the entire surface of his hands to knead his way slowly back to her neck. *That feels sooooo good.* "Most people still believe in the scare tactic, catching someone by surprise." He began to work on her nape…into her hairline…behind her ears… "I've never found that to be effective. Have you?"

She responded with something that sounded vaguely like, "Mmm-nnnnrrfflephlumph," and didn't trouble herself to clarify. He palmed the back of her head, his fingers pressing circles into her scalp like a hat with benefits. Nothing, *nothing* had ever felt this good, except…

Except for the last time he'd touched her with this kind of freedom. Well, more than this kind of freedom. Last time, he had touched her naked body, and relaxation wasn't quite the release they'd been after.

Well on her way to cooked-noodle state, Rosemary couldn't summon even a smidge of alarm over that thought. Why had touching never felt this good before? She'd been married, and for the ten years, everything had been hunky-dory—from her perspective. She'd had no complaints about sex, either the frequency or the intensity. Although…

In comparison to the fireworks Dean's lovemaking had set off, her ex-husband was more of a…sparkler.

Desire had crashed upon her like a tsunami when she and Dean were on the dance floor. Her body had needed him, or so it had seemed at the time, the way bread needed flour to exist. *Don't dance with him, not ever again,* she'd commanded herself the morning after.

Dimly she realized that letting him massage her was not in line with her decision *never to lose control again.* But this massage wasn't about tsunami-like sexual heat. No, no, it was…gentle. Relaxing. Platonic, right?

His hands made a return trip down her spine, stopping to work an extra minute on her lower back. As she was wearing a dress rather than pants, Dean did not need to fight a waistband in order for his magic fingers to press and knead, working into her hips. A haze of sensation dulled Rosemary's thoughts until they felt about as fluid as oatmeal.

Never felt sooo good…

Do… Not… Stop, she thought.

"I won't," Dean whispered back.

Oops.

When his palms slipped up her back like smoke, Rosemary leaned into them. She didn't mean to, really… Although she didn't exactly mean *not* to. Regardless of how she tried to care about the future and about not being weak or impulsive, she couldn't seem to access the principles her mother and sisters wore like a second skin.

True to his promise, Dean did not stop massaging. When he tilted her neck, pressing his thumb and fingers along the stiff muscles, cupping her jaw in a palm as warm and soothing as a summer day, Rosemary sighed and leaned into the caress. She turned her head to say, "Thank you," but no words emerged. Instead they locked gazes, and the words she should have spoken became a kiss she should not have given.

Really should not have.

Should not have brought her hand up to reach for his neck and pull him closer…

Should not have moaned into his lips as she tasted him for the first time in months.

This was what had stunned her so the night they'd gotten together, this hunger. It made her feel alive, strong. It made her feel daring and bold and free. And she'd never felt that way, not even as a kid. Life had always been a field filled with land mines to avoid. Caution had to be exercised, and her family's brand of caution generally involved "healthy cynicism," which translated to "Trust no one."

But none of that mattered now, with Dean. As the eddying sensation pulled her deeper and deeper to its center, Rosemary knew the physical spell he cast was not the sole reason she was abandoning her cloak of protection; she couldn't ignore the way he interacted with his family, his Mr. Rogers naturalness with children....

Bet you never wanted to shag Mr. Rogers, though, did you?

It was Dean who brought them face-to-face. And Dean who pulled back long enough to look into her eyes, to make sure she knew that this was no mere indiscriminate lust, not on his part.

He began kissing her again, his mouth hot and ravenous, and soon they were lying on his couch, their legs tangling discourteously, her hands running up his sides and traveling across his back as she noted for the first time that he'd ditched the lab coat.

Rosemary's breasts tightened and tingled even before his hand found the generous mounds. As he touched her, managing to tease her nipples through her thin dress and lacy bra, she thought she might levitate off the couch.

She began to yank his shirt from his trousers, needing to feel his skin...needing, really, to feel his skin on her skin... and recognizing the precise moment when she decided she couldn't stop, wasn't going to stop until the sharp, painful ache inside her had been soothed—

Then, suddenly, it was over.

Rosemary wasn't sure what had happened at first. Her eyes were closed, so all she knew was that one moment her body felt like an inferno with a gasoline drip and the next moment she was cold, floundering, wondering what was wrong.

She opened her eyelids with extreme effort, blinked at the light coming through the windows on the other side of the apartment and saw Dean sitting up, one of his hands on her tummy as if he required the continuity, his chest rising and falling visibly as he panted his way back to normal.

When he was sufficiently recovered, he helped her sit, straightened her dress at the shoulders and with a small smile noted, "This probably isn't a good way to kick off a celibate marriage." Running first one hand then the other through his hair, he expelled a breath filled with pent-up energy. "How are those hiccups?"

Rosemary figured her options at this moment were a) embarrassment, b) relief or c) frustration. Since she'd always been rotten at multiple choice, she aimed merely for coherent. "Fine." Her voice sounded hoarse and thready. "Gone." Attempting an urbane laugh, she said, "I think you found a new cure."

"I doubt it's new." Reaching out, he looped one of her curls around his forefinger. "Effective, though." Hovering on the brink of speaking again, he changed his mind, released her hair and stood. "I'll take a look at that document after work." Again she had the sense he had something more on his mind.

Rosemary couldn't regroup nearly as quickly as he seemed able to and stood more slowly. Lucy had told her to tell Dean something about the prenup, but what was it…? She frowned. Oh, yeah—

"Um, my sister wanted me to mention something that's a bit different from what we discussed. About the marriage. A little detail."

"Oh. Uh-huh." Dean cleared his throat. "Yeah…. Changes— they happen."

"Yes."

His tie had loosened during their…activity…and yet he tugged on it now as if it was choking him. "In fact, I was going to talk to you about… I wanted to mention…" He shook his head. "What's the change?"

Rosemary stared at him. Up to now he'd always seemed enviably sure of himself. "What do you want to ask?"

"What's the change in the prenuptial agreement?"

"Oh, it's not actually written into the prenup. It's part of our verbal agreement…about the length of time we're going to be together. Married."

His brows rose abruptly then swooped lower than before as he awaited elaboration.

Rosemary hadn't thought the change would be a problem since this marriage was destined to have a short shelf life from the get-go, but now anxiety fizzed inside her.

Silly. It's not going to matter. Just tell him. "Well, originally, we agreed to one and a half years of marriage from our wedding day, if you remember? But Lucy said the divorce might be smoother if we stick it out two years. I think she considers two years some kind of magic number for proving you gave the marriage the old college try." Rosemary swooped her fist through the air. *Cute. That made you look like an idiot.* Dropping the smile and her hand, she shrugged at him. "Are you okay with that?"

Dean lowered his head and pressed two fingers to his eyes. Imminent migraine. Probably not a good sign. Although he was the one who'd been pro-marriage from the start, anything could have changed since they'd spoken about it. Maybe it appeared to him that she was trying to manipulate their agreement to her advantage, which…well, she was. Sighing, Rosemary told herself to be prepared if he was perturbed.

Despite that note to self, she was *not* prepared when Dean started laughing. Laughing.

"What?" she asked, watching him warily. *Was that ha-ha-funny laughter or demonic "I'll be damned if I let you screw with my life, sister," laughter?* "Um, look, if it's not going to work for you, just say so, because it was Lucy's idea, anyway. She's probably just being extracautious. She's like that. Personally, I think it's a little silly to assume that a few more months—"

Dean sobered abruptly. "It's Lucy's idea?" Looking away, he nodded to himself, wiping a hand down the face that only seconds before was wreathed in laughter. "You, of course, would have preferred not to add six more months to this marriage." He didn't wait for her to answer. Rising as if he were very tired, he walked around the sofa, grabbed his lab coat and shrugged into it. "Two years suits me fine. Another six months in the same house with my child—can't argue with that, can I?" He smiled, but it failed to reach his eyes. "I'll be happy to sign."

Rosemary didn't know how to respond, which seemed to be a continual state for her lately.

"You want me to bring the papers to you or send them to your sister?" he asked.

"Whatever you're comfortable with."

Without telling her what that would be, he crossed to the door, leaving Rosemary still buzzing with lust and confusion.

With empty eyes, Dean gave her a brief nod. "I've got to get back to work. Come down when you're ready. Just pull the door shut on your way out."

Chapter Ten

Things moved fairly quickly after that. Dean sent the signed prenuptial agreement directly to Lucy, who texted Rosemary, "He signed. 0 changes. Lucky U."

Rosemary applied herself to her work at the library, but her mind never strayed far from the realization that it wouldn't take long for her pregnancy to show, so if she and Dean planned to go public as a couple, it would behoove them to do it sooner rather than later.

Even though there was a family physician right here in Honeyford, Rosemary had begun seeing an ob-gyn in Bend. Perhaps after she and Dean came out of the closet (or bedroom?), so to speak, she would change doctors and save herself the drive.

Listening to the library's grandfather clock chime noon, Rosemary reached for one of the peppermints she kept in her drawer at the reference desk. Thus far on her list of fun ways to spend the day, pregnancy and salmonella were running neck and neck.

Nearing the end of her first trimester, she expected her morning sickness to abate. That was what the books she'd purchased from Amazon suggested (Dean still had the library's best pregnancy guides). Unfortunately, Rosemary's nausea had increased in the past few days, and now it seemed to be a loyal companion. Gone were the ravenous nights that allowed her to fill up on the food she couldn't even squint at during the day. She'd lost a pound this week.

No one stopped by the library on his lunch hour to wave a pastrami sandwich under her nose, either. She hadn't seen or heard from Dean for several days, not since she'd dropped off the prenuptial agreement.

Interestingly, just thinking about their romp on the couch ignited inside her an inferno of sexual heat that temporarily burned off the nausea. And made her hiccup.

"Are you hiccuping *again?*" Her clerk, Abby, joined her at the reference desk. Abby's wardrobe changed along with her choice in reading material. Currently she was devouring *The Catcher in the Rye* at Rosemary's suggestion and had replaced the 1940s shoulder pads with a pearl-buttoned sweater set, full skirt and saddle shoes. "You should get those hiccups checked out," she said. "My boyfriend's brother hiccuped for thirty-five days straight and didn't stop until they took him to the hospital."

"What did the hospital do for him?"

Abby helped herself to a mint. "They ran a CAT scan and found out he'd swallowed a quarter at his cousin's bar mitzvah."

A shiver of alarm pattered up Rosemary's back. *Hic.* "That's what was causing him to hiccup?"

Working the mint around her mouth, Abby shrugged. "Doubtful. He'd gone to the bar mitzvah two years earlier. Good to know there was a quarter in there, though. I think they operated. I'll ask. In the meantime, want me to scare you?"

"You just did." *Hic.* "I'm going to refill my water bottle."

"Okay. Oh!" Reaching into the folds of her pink skirt, Abby withdrew an envelope. "Here. For you."

Rosemary accepted the square linen envelope, noting her name—and nothing more—printed neatly on the front. "Where'd you get this?"

"My friend Polly brought it by when she came to drop off books."

"Polly?" Frowning, Rosemary tried to remember if she'd met a Polly in town.

"She's in high school with my cousin Emily. Polly works at the pharmacy."

The tips of Rosemary's fingers began to itch with the desire to rip open the envelope. Controlling herself, she shrugged her eyebrows and said, "Hmm." *Look at me, all indifferent.*

Forcing herself to toss—not place carefully, but actually toss—the envelope next to the keyboard on her desk, as if she wasn't the least bit curious, Rosemary feigned a businesslike glance at her watch.

"Why don't you take lunch now," she suggested. "I'll hold down the fort until story hour."

"Okay. Cool. I brought leftovers, so I'll be in the back, reading, if you need me."

Rosemary sat calmly until Abby was out of eyesight and then, because no one else was nearby, she fumbled the envelope open with shaky fingers and pulled out a simple ivory card with an embossed *K* at the top. She hiccuped once before she read the message:

Rosemary,
Hoping you will join me for dinner tomorrow evening
at the Honeyford Inn, 7 p.m. Regrets only.
Dean

Above the too-rapid beat of her heart, Rosemary reread the inked lines. This was the first time she'd seen Dean's handwriting—clear, bold letters, not too fancy yet with a distinct style. He'd drawn a small happy face after "Regrets only."

This was also the first time he had formally invited her on a date.

Rosemary's hand wandered to her tummy. She patted the baby. "Sorry we've done this backward, sweetie pie. Mama has never had a good sense of direction where men are concerned."

Her breath caught in her throat almost painfully as she realized another first: the first time she referred to herself as Mama. the image of herself holding a baby with hair as soft as kitten fur, teensy fingers with teensy nails and toes that looked like bay shrimp filled her with a flood of emotion that made tears spring to her eyes. Instantly, however, worry chased the love. Her mind began to reel with *What if* and *Oh, no* statements.

What if she had a daughter, and her wonderful, beautiful, tenderhearted girl had the same rotten luck with men that Rosemary, her mother and sisters had? *Oh, no!*

What if she had a son, and he sensed that his mother was weak, confused and cynical about men? *Oh, no!*

What if she and Dean disagreed about parenting techniques, and their child grew up confused, angry and disillusioned? *Oh, no, no, no!*

The nausea returned so strongly Rosemary was sorry she'd told Abby to take her break.

Scrabbling for the peppermints again, she sucked air like

a fish in cloudy water. This settled it: she had to establish a good relationship with Dean. One that was open, mutually respectful and, above all else, sane. The youngest of her sisters, Rosemary didn't remember their father at all, but Lucy had once purchased two Siamese fighting fish, housing them in a small bowl with a clear divider. The fish would puff their fins and glare at each other as if they'd like to bust through the plastic separating them and rip each other's heads off. Lucy had named them Mom and Dad.

"And look what happened to us," Rosemary muttered, wondering what her patrons would think if she put her head between her knees to calm the dizziness.

Slipping Dean's card into the pocket of her cardigan, she knew they would need to talk, to map out exactly how they planned to parent, how to conduct their relationship, and precisely how to end it when the time came. And they needed to arrive at these understandings quickly, before they could harm their child in any way. Nothing should be left to chance or the whims of the day.

It began to occur to Rosemary that life was handing her an opportunity she had given up on completely—the chance to be someone's mother and to do it well.

A sense of wonder began to rush like an un-dammed river through her veins. She had already resigned herself to reading *The Dr. Seuss Sleep Book* during library story hour, but never with a sleepy, pajama-covered bundle of her own tucked beneath her arm. She'd stopped imagining making animal-cracker zoos and Lego Ferris wheels. Out of a sense of self-preservation, she had changed her goals and told herself it was…okay. Now the dreams she had relegated to the discard pile could be pulled out again.

Where nausea had dominated only moments before, Rosemary now felt like a balloon, so filled with joy she might pop. She covered her belly with both hands.

"It's going to be so good, sweet darling baby. You're going to have the best life. And you don't have to worry about your father and me. We'll find a way to do this so everyone gets along." Her promise was a solemn whisper. "We'll never, ever, ever hurt you."

The Honeyford Inn occupied a three-story brick building downtown. Hotel rooms comprised the top floor, with a restaurant serving Eastern European cuisine making up the main and lower levels.

Rosemary had heard the food was excellent and was actually looking forward to her evening with Dean. In fact, she hadn't felt as queasy today and was hungry as a bear.

After work yesterday, she'd driven over an hour to Bend, where she'd hit every major store selling anything related to babies, children, pregnant women or parenting. Onesies and adorable knit hats, a doll-size snowsuit in fire-engine red, a Boppy pillow for breast-feeding, Winnie the Pooh bookends and the most current parenting books filled the shopping bags she had lugged to her car.

She hadn't been able to resist the maternity stores, either, and handed the maître d' her coat to reveal her first maternity-related purchase for herself—a silky, V-necked dress in variegated swirls of hot pink and red. The dress had a stretchy tummy panel (so cute!) and a gorgeous drape. The extra folds of material looked fabulous now and would expand as necessary to accommodate her growing belly. Her budget took a hit when she wrote the check to Angel Kisses Maternity for a garment she didn't strictly *need* yet, but it was worth it. Oh, mama, was it worth it! This dress was a celebration.

"Your party is waiting for you in the cellar," the maître d' informed her formally.

Rosemary followed him down a short staircase to "the cellar," a wonderful room with brick walls, thick wood pillars and five linen-cloaked tables, each a comfortable distance from the next, providing an eminently private and cozy setting. There was even a fire snapping in the wood-burning fireplace.

Dean rose as Rosemary approached.

A twinge of anxiety threatened as she wondered if he was still upset about the prenup, but the look in his eyes calmed her.

"You look...stunning."

His expression reflected every woman's dream response to her dolling-up efforts. His gaze took in her hair, her face, the dress, and his slow-spreading smile made her feel like the only woman in the room even though every table was filled with diners.

"You look nice, too. I like your suit."

He smoothed his tie. Dean looked, she thought, like an ad for Yves St. Laurent for men. Compliments traded, they sat. Rosemary told herself that all she had to do tonight was enjoy the company of the man she had, on one fateful night, found too delicious to resist. Tonight she would be cordial, engaging, interested, but a whole lot calmer. And, of course, she'd keep her clothes on this time, because they were in public, and she didn't want another episode like the one in his apartment.

It was a good plan, and it didn't even sound that difficult. All she had to do was keep a clear head.

Accepting the wine list, Dean lifted a brow at his dinner companion. No alcoholic beverages for her, though they were the only two people present who knew why. Dean hoped she would let him rectify that tonight. He'd done a lot of thinking since their kiss on his couch, and now he had a goal and a plan. It was time to go public with their relationship.

After they ordered drinks and dinner, he kept the conversation light and upbeat, telling her about Honeyford's illustrious history (founded by a family of Italian beekeepers named

Castigliano, many of whom were terrified of bees), the up-coming spring festival—Honeyford Days—and the fact that his limelight-loathing little brother had been roped into being Grand Marshal.

"Fletcher was in the rodeo. Back then he was meaner than some of the bulls he rode, but he's got a movie-star puss the women loved. He wound up doing clothing ads, a few TV commercials. He'd signed on for a role in a movie, a Western, before he had an accident that laid him up for months and finally brought him back home."

"Wait a minute." Rosemary sat back from the bread pudding she'd made a sizable dent in. "Fletcher Kingsley is your brother? Fletcher Kingsley, the Tuff Enuff jeans model?"

Dean winced. "Yeah, let's not refer to him as a 'model' at family gatherings like Thanksgiving or Christmas, though, okay?" He winked. "Best to keep peace in the family."

"Okay, but you have to let me get a signed photo for my friend Vi. She set her TiVo for those jeans commercials."

He laughed then lowered his voice way, way down. "You seem to be feeling better. How's the morning sickness?"

Rosemary didn't seem to mind the topic change. "Better since yesterday."

"Good. According to the book, it gets better after the first trimester, and you're almost there."

"You're still reading the book?"

"I like to follow along, imagine where you're at." Again, he'd spoken softly and was pleased to see that she didn't mind the references to her pregnancy.

"I do feel a hundred percent better," Rosemary offered, spooning up another taste of the custard sauce beneath the bread pudding. "I went shopping in Bend last night as a matter of fact and ate at The Olive Garden. I'm not even going to think about how many breadsticks I had." She leaned over the table and smiled in a way that made Dean's heart skip.

"Maternity clothes have this fabulous expandable panel in the front. All pants should be made that way."

He glanced toward the couple at the table closest to them. The Marsdens had greeted Dean when they'd first arrived twenty minutes earlier. Currently they were occupied with the pierogi appetizer and appeared no more interested in Dean's conversation with Rosemary than Dean and Rosemary were in the pierogis.

Dean knew, however, that he was about to make them much, much more interested. He crossed his fingers that he was doing the right thing.

"More coffee?" The word emerged hoarsely. *Damn.* When was the last time he'd been nervous? Couldn't remember. Clearing his throat, he tried again. "Coffee?"

Setting her spoon on her plate, Rosie leaned back in her chair and held up a hand. "Lord, no, I'm stuffed to the gills. Making up for lost time, I guess. Everything was delicious."

"Here we are." Holding a silver tray, Josef and Annette, owners of the Honeyford Inn, approached the table. "A special dessert, just for you." With great care, Annette set before Rosie a china plate with a thick square of darkest chocolate topped by a marzipan rose. A gold ribbon bow sat on the edge of the plate.

Rosie looked at the creation with something approaching alarm, but recovered well and smiled charmingly at the pair that hovered over the table. "It's beautiful. Did you make it here?"

"Yes!" Annette nodded eagerly. "One of a kind. With a surprise inside."

"Mama, shh." Josef patted Annette on the arm then pointed a gnarled finger at the plate. "Taste." He waggled his thick gray brows.

Dean grimaced. Subtle as a sledgehammer.

Rosie looked slightly sick at the thought of more dessert.

"That dinner was *so* fabulous, and the bread pudding was amazing. I don't think I have room for anything else right now." She lifted the plate to hand it across the table. "Maybe Dean—"

"No!" Josef and Annette both stretched out a hand. Startled, Rosemary clunked the plate back onto the table.

Dean narrowed his eyes at the duo.

"We want *you* to try it." Josef looked at her appealingly. "Dean, he's been coming here since he was young. It will mean more if you tell us how *you* like it."

"Oh. Well…I suppose there's always room for a tiny bite." Picking up the small silver fork sitting on the plate, she sliced a piece of the dense chocolate and chewed obligingly. Her smile was only a little strained. "Delicious."

Josef looked worried. "No, eat the rose."

Dean shook his head. "Maybe you could give us a minute—"

But Rosie was already dutifully forking up a marzipan petal and raising it to her lips. "Mmm." She looked as if she could barely swallow. Once she'd managed the feat, she set down the fork and sat back. "It's a lovely dessert. Are you putting it on the menu?"

Annette and Josef looked at each other in grave concern. Annette began to wring her hands. They both turned to Dean.

It was hardly the way he'd envisioned the moment. Reaching for the plate, he pulled it toward him. Nestled amidst the formed flowers, was the object of the whole dessert. He plucked it out of the marzipan, stood and didn't even bother to try to exile Annette and Joseph.

"Excuse me," he said, shouldering past them. When he reached Rosie, he knelt. Her eyes turned into huge hazel moons as he held the ruby ring out to her.

"It's taken my entire adult life—and no small part of my

adolescence—to find you," he began. "I've imagined what life would be like with a woman who was my best friend, my partner in all that's good and my bulwark against the tough times. I've imagined what it would be like to be that person for someone else, and I've never trusted that I could be, not a hundred percent. Until now."

He reached for one of her hands, resting limply in her lap while she gaped at him. Holding her fingers and the ring, he gazed steadily into her eyes, unmindful of the whispers that circled the room.

"Rosemary Josephine Jeffers," he said, "will you be that woman, that partner and friend, and allow me to be yours? Will you believe in me when the going is rough and trust that I believe in you, too? Because more than anything in my life right now, I would like to be your husband." He took a breath and hit the bull's-eye. "Will you marry me?"

Josef sniffled. The room went utterly silent, save for a watery "Awww" in the background. Dean's heart pounded the seconds as he awaited a response from the woman who appeared, currently, like a photograph taken immediately after someone had jumped out and yelled, "Surprise!"

Well, he thought, swallowing around a knot in his throat that felt as if he'd overtightened his tie, *that went well.*

The first time a man had asked her to marry him, she'd choked on a pepperoni. Choked in joy, of course.

Rosemary had been dating Neil for three-and-a-half years. At the time of the proposal, he'd been preparing for his second year of law school, and she had recently packed all her worldly goods to move to Seattle, where she was going to earn her Master's degree in Library and Information Sciences.

"Maybe we should get married," Neil had said over a large pie—half pepperoni and green pepper for her, half kitchen sink for him (if only she'd realized then that he had trouble discriminating).

"I'm leaving for U of W in two weeks," she had protested (admittedly weakly) once the pepperoni had gone down. Washington had one of the top-ranked Library Sciences programs in the country. She'd been planning since high school to get her degree there. She'd had an apartment, her student loans and a part-time job at a local public library all lined up. Neil had known that. They'd talked about it, talked about how they would navigate a long-distance relationship.

"You can get your Master's in Portland." His goofy smile had massaged the cavalier comment into something romantic, daring almost. *Give up your plans for me, baby. Love will make it worth the while.*

And she had seen it then, if she'd been honest enough to admit it—his fear that the "the long-distance thing" would not work. He had known he would stray.

At the time, however, Rosemary had told herself Neil couldn't wait to marry her, that he was itching to be a family man. She'd insisted to herself and her sisters and mother that true love really did exist and that marriage wouldn't hold them back; it would be the wind beneath their wings.

It hadn't even bothered her that her student loans had not transferred, that she'd wound up working full-time in the Multnomah County Public Library System—first shelving books and then as a clerk—while she went to school, that she had developed migraines, or that she'd slept an average of four hours a night for two years. What difference did any of that make, she'd told herself, in the long run? She and Neil were bound to start a family soon, anyway; she'd be staying home for several years once their first baby arrived since no way was she going to repeat her own childhood. She would get her degree now and use it in the future.

She and Neil had gone ring shopping together and purchased

what they could afford at the time—Black Hills Gold bands
with a diamond chip for each of them. He'd lost his on a
river-rafting trip (white water, after all) before their second
anniversary. She had cherished hers until the day she'd taken
it off for good.

Now, a good decade after that first proposal, she stared at
what appeared to be a diamond-crusted platinum band with a
heart-shaped ruby nestled in the center. *Yowza*. Unless Dean's
morning cereal had come with an unusually good piece of
costume jewelry, this was the real deal, and it was a ring like
nothing she had ever imagined on her finger. The only thing
that brought the confection down to earth was the marzipan
gumming up one row of tiny prong-set diamonds.

"Will you..." he had just asked on bended knee. With a
great preamble.

What he had not said: *Will you marry me, Rosemary Jeffers, mother of the baby we did not plan, even though we've
already agreed we're going to divorce before we've picked
out a preschool?*

He knew and she knew they were going to get married; he
needn't have bothered with the trappings of a proposal.

A muffled whimper cut through Rosemary's thoughts, and
she glanced beyond Dean to Annette, who clutched Josef's
hand and compressed her lips so as not to sob out loud.

Unlocked, Rosemary's gaze traveled the intimate, candlelit
room to see that the customers at all five tables in the Honeyford Inn's cellar were glued to the action as if it were the
final rose ceremony on *The Bachelorette*.

Surely the news would travel upstairs to the main dining
room before the end of the evening. By tomorrow more and
more people would know that the hometown pharmacist had
proposed to Honeyford's new librarian as prettily as any man
deeply in love.

And suddenly Rosemary realized: he'd done it this way to

get the ball rolling. By the time people discovered she was pregnant, the myth that she and Dean loved each other to distraction would be the stuff of local legend. Their child could grow up in Honeyford and never hear that he or she had been "an accident."

She looked again at the man who knelt before her. In the dim light Dean's blue eyes looked like a calm sea, steady and eternal. *Take your time,* his gaze told her. *I'm not going anywhere.*

Surely she was supposed to speak now. A small dining-roomful of people waited for her to complete this über-romantic moment. But über-romantic dialogue required some emotional investment, and she had no idea what her emotions were at present. Was it normal to feel numb and sort of dazed and that was all when a man said all the right things and then presented you with a ring that would rock the world of any girl who had grown up staging and restaging her engagement with Barbie dolls?

Finally Rosemary had a good proposal with which to entertain her children and grandchildren. Dean's proposal was one she could recite again by heart for their fiftieth anniversary party at the Governor Hotel in downtown Portland. It was a proposal from which tender excerpts could be culled for inclusion on side-by-side tombstones.

Damned shame that none of it was real.

Probably fewer than thirty seconds rolled by, during which Dean remained calm and charitably patient, but a quiet murmur arose in the peanut gallery. "Did she hear him?" someone whispered.

She knew she should respond immediately, but…

This could be my last—and best—proposal. I should at least know what I feel.

Gratitude. She felt grateful that he'd wrapped their child—and her, as well—in a gauzy fairy tale, for the time being anyway. Maybe it wasn't very forthright or very modern, and perhaps Oprah would frown, but she'd rather have people gossip about her whirlwind courtship than her one-night stand.

Besides gratitude, she felt…affection, actually. Dean Kingsley had taken this entire situation better than most men would have. He was kind. And he had integrity.

And besides gratitude and affection, there was that feeling of lust that kept cropping up, especially when she looked at his ears. It was weird, her reaction to those ears, but he had longish earlobes. Longish earlobes that had felt velvety when she'd nibbled on them back in December. There was something about long lobes that said *stability*. You could grow old with them.

For an instant an image slashed across her mind. Two old people, one with curly gray hair and one with long ears, sitting on the porch of a sweet two-story house with dormers, a stone chimney and a birdhouse they'd made themselves hanging from the branch of an oak tree. The old couple laughed as they reminisced….

"Remember when Montana told the neighbor boy she had a magic hat that made people fly, and they climbed onto the roof to test it out?"

"Remember how Nate used to sit under the oak tree with Buster and tell that old dog all his secrets?"

Oh, my gosh, they even had an old dog….

There was a for-sale sign on the front lawn, because now that it was just the two of them, they were moving to something smaller. Their new place still had a formal dining room, though—she'd insisted on that—for big family Thanksgivings and Christmases. And on the wall of their new living room they intended to hang a photo of the house that had held their family so sweetly during the growing-up years….

Swallowed tears put a lump in Rosemary's throat.

She looked at Dean, so calm, so steady, and her foolish heart began to hope.

What if she was getting one more chance at forever? Maybe…just maybe…this time—

Hic.

Oh, no.

Hic-hic. Oh, holy heaven. She slapped a hand to her breastbone. Her worst case of hiccups yet began the assault on her diaphragm. *Hic-hic-hic.*

"Rosie?" Dean's expression, previously the picture of forbearance, began to exhibit some tension. "You all right?"

Her eyes bugged at Dean. Poor Dean. This was not a proper response at all. "I'm fine—" *Hic.* "Ow. Maybe a little water—" *Hic-hic.* Ohhh, why did she eat the whole bread pudding? Every hiccup felt like a blender churning the contents of her stomach.

"Push under her ribs, once. Hard," Josef instructed as Dean stood.

"That's for choking." Annette slapped her husband's arm. "She should suck on a hard candy while drinking a glass of water with one tablespoon of cider vinegar. I'll get it."

Rosemary groaned. "No—" *Hic-hic.*

Dean put a hand on her shoulder. It was warm and comforting. "Is another massage in order?" he whispered, a brow hooked.

She hiccuped in his face.

"Have her jump up and down on one leg and—"

"She should sing the national anthem while—"

"Put your fingers in your ears and hold your breath for a full minute."

Pelted by advice, Rosemary's head began to ache as much as her stomach. Only the hand on her shoulder provided relief, and she wanted to lean into it, to rest against the body in front of her. She was tired. All the worries and uncertainty and secrecy of the past few weeks had been exhausting. Was Dean exhausted? Her eyes met his. He cocked his head.

Oh, Dean. Poor, poor Dean. He had publicly proposed and earned a spate of hiccups in response. She looked for the ring in his free hand, prepared to give him the public acceptance he deserved. He really was a gentleman, a decent person, a—

Hic!

A glass of water was lifted to her lips. Dean again. Gratefully, she took long, breath-stealing gulps and then waited a moment. Calm. *There. Now please let that be the end of it.* She pushed the glass aside. Where was the ring?

"Dean." She focused on his eyes. Kind and, yes, honest eyes. "Dean, I—"

Abruptly, droplets of sweat popped onto her forehead and above her upper lip and then…pretty much everywhere else very quickly. Rosemary had a sudden mental image of the food in her stomach looking like dozens of crazed beavers building a dam against white water. Her hands went round her middle.

Hold on, Rosemary. Just hold on. The man deserves a proper response.

"Dean." She shoved a smile to her lips. "I…I… Uh-oh."

The restroom was on the main level of the restaurant, ten steps up from the cellar.

Rosemary wasted no time. She made a run for it, leaving behind a roomful of spectators and Dean, who doubtless would remember this moment for the rest of his days.

It looked as if the second proposal she'd received in her life was going to be even harder to put a spin on than the first.

"Rosemary, it's Dean. I'm coming in."

Too busy to argue, Rosemary continued giving up her dinner as Dean entered the women's room. Unoccupied save for the pathetic barfing pregnant woman, the bathroom was not, alas, as soundproof as Rosemary would have wished. She heard the clinking of china and glasses and the hum of the diners. Then, directly behind her, came Dean's softly uttered swear.

"Aw, Rosie…"

He held her hair, stroked her back then brought her a moist paper towel. Any embarrassment Rosemary might have suffered dissipated beneath the quilt of comforting murmurs and Dean's immensely soothing back rub.

Who knew how many minutes passed before he asked, "Is it always this bad?"

Rosemary shook her head, dabbing her brow with the towel as she leaned against the sink. "Days aren't great, but I stick to crackers and toast so I can't get too sick." Folding the damp paper, she tossed it in the trash. "Nights are usually fine."

"Unless you're proposed to?" His voice was rich with irony, but devoid of anger.

"Oh, my. You really are a nice man," she said softly, surprising a wince out of him.

"Rosie—"

"No, truly. I…I can see that, and I'm sorry I've made things so difficult."

"Rosie, I need—"

"I accept your proposal." She made a face. "Obviously I accept it. I mean, we planned it, but…you didn't have to do it this way, with so much thoughtfulness, and I appreciate it."

"Yeah. Ro—"

"Unless, of course, you want to rescind it after all this." She laughed, but became acutely aware that every part of her, every tiny little part of her, hoped he would say, *Hell no, I'm not rescinding anything.*

Good golly crackers, she truly was starting to believe in him. Maybe she'd begun to believe in him a while ago, and that accounted for the nerves—

"Oh, my gosh," she realized suddenly. "I'm not hiccuping." She blinked at the realization, waiting to be sure. "They're gone. I'm accepting a marriage proposal to a genuinely nice man, and I'm not hiccuping!" The hope she'd squashed so ruthlessly began to peek through her season of disillusionment, like the sun finding it's way through a break in the clouds.

Dean arched a brow. "This is progress, I take it?"

She nodded and whispered, "This is progress."

Some expression she couldn't identify lingered until at last his gaze cleared to azure blue. He reached a hand into his coat pocket.

In the modest but homey ladies' room of the Honeyford Inn, Dean proposed to Rosemary again, without the bended knee and tender words this time (they really did need to get out of the bathroom), yet Rosemary felt more content accepting him than she'd ever imagined she could be.

Slipping the ring on her finger, he said, "I guessed at the size. And the gemstone."

She ought to have protested a ring so costly, particularly when theirs was a union with start-stop dates. If the marriage ended—*when* the marriage ended—she would give the ring back to him, but for now, after upchucking at his first attempt to formally propose, Rosemary was determined to be gracious. "I think rubies are lovely. So different."

"We began differently." He held her hand, the low lights making the heart-shaped stone glow warmly. "Maybe we'll end on an up note."

Or, Rosemary thought for the first time, shocked when she didn't freak out at the thought, *maybe we won't end at all.*

They exited the restroom together, and Rosemary was stunned to find a group of people from the cellar waiting for them, plus most of the upstairs diners turned their way to see what the fuss was about.

"Isn't that the new librarian?"

"Really? Was she drinking?"

"So did she say yes or no?" asked one of the women from the cellar. "I didn't hear."

Rosemary felt her left hand clasped and squeezed. She glanced up.

Dean smiled, just for her. His upstage eye closed in a private wink. Then, turning toward the dining room, he raised their hands for everyone to see. The ruby ring drew wide-eyed stares. And a gasp from Annette.

"You're looking at the luckiest man in the world," he said.

Annette's sweet face crumpled as she burst into happy tears. She and Josef embraced. "In our restaurant," he blubbered, patting his wife's back.

Applause erupted from the small crowd gathered outside the bathroom and "Congratulations!" echoed around the dining room.

Rosemary couldn't help it: she started to cry, too…because everyone was so sweet, and because Dean sounded so sincere and because, if only in this moment, she was able to set aside the facts surrounding her engagement and focus on the feelings. And what she felt—even if it would only be for this one moment—was like the world's luckiest woman.

Chapter Eleven

"You're playing with fire."

Fletcher leaned against the outer wall of a horse stall, eating his pecan roll while Dean viciously stabbed clean hay with a pitchfork.

"I know it," Dean growled, spreading the straw around the interior of the stall. "Don't you think I know that?"

Fletcher shrugged. "If you know it then why are you here shoveling hay instead of coming clean about the will with Rosemary? And what is it about my ranch chores that attract you when you're hiding out? Not that I'm complaining." Lifting a red Honey Bea's travel mug, he took a long pull of coffee.

"I need the physical outlet." Dean pushed the words through gritted teeth. "I can't release tension counting pills."

"Understandable." Fletcher swirled the coffee inside the mug. "According to Claire, half the town is babbling about your engagement. Very romantic and all that crap. You might have been better off keeping things private if you're not going to tell Rosemary the truth. Keep things a little more low-key to spare her feelings in the long run."

"Thanks for the tip, Dr. Phil." Dean took another ferocious stab at the hay. "How many people know about the will?"

"Aside from you and me?" Fletcher popped the rest of the pecan roll in his mouth and thought. "Claire, of course. Gwen."

Dean nodded. Their father's mistress was the mayor of Honeyford and the executor of Victor's will. Fortunately, Gwen was also an eminently reasonable woman. She believed the marriage codicil to be a huge mistake. Although she loved Honeyford and had numerous plans to bring more revenue to the often-struggling town, she did not want to feather Honeyford's nest with Fletcher or Dean's inheritance. She'd sold Pine Road Ranch back to Fletcher for a dollar.

Dean stopped working and backhanded sweat off his brow. "I approached Gwen about buying the building on Main if I default on the will. She thinks she'll get resistance from the city council. You were right—Doug Thorpe's been badgering the city to buy up stores and find lessees with upscale businesses. He's not going to go for a low-cost, bilingual medical clinic."

Fletcher nodded. "So why aren't you telling Rosemary the truth? That inheriting the building is going to benefit people who sorely need a medical clinic."

Dean sighed, feeling out of touch with himself for perhaps the first time in his life. "I planned to. The morning after I proposed. After I made it clear to the town how I feel about her, so there won't be any question about why we're marrying." Fletcher would understand that. He had been bound and determined not to allow any demeaning gossip to affect his wife on account of the blasted will. "I was going to tell her about the will and the clinic and then let her know that I'm going to forfeit the building, because I don't want that hanging over our heads for the next two years. I want to make this marriage work. I need this family to work."

"So what happened?" Fletcher asked.

"I got a letter." Dean rubbed the back of his neck. He was working on a forty-eight-hour headache ibuprofen hadn't been able to touch. "From a doctor who wants to help open and then work in the clinic."

"I didn't know you'd started recruiting already."

"I haven't," Dean said. "I've been working on grants. She found out about it from an aunt who knows Alberto."

"She. The doc is a woman?"

"Esmeralda Duran. Her mother is Guatemalan. Father's Spanish. Esmeralda trained as an EMT then went to UC Irvine for her medical degree. She's coming off two years of volunteer work in Guatemala."

"Speaks Spanish then."

"Fluently. Wrote eloquently about how she wants to support the community not only with medical aid, but also education. She heard about Clinica Adelina from an aunt who lives in the area. The aunt heard about it from Alberto."

Fletcher whistled. "Perfect. But if you default on the will…"

"I'll have no building. I've got a real-estate agent combing the area for something suitable."

"But you'll have to buy the building or pay rent."

"Right. It'll be a setback, not one I'm sure we can conquer soon. How do I tell Alberto the plans are on hold, indefinitely? And how do I turn away a doctor who can make it all come together?"

"By keeping your mouth shut, getting married to the mother of your child and hoping she'll understand when the truth comes out?"

Grimacing, Dean nodded slowly. "That might be my plan," he admitted.

Fletcher wagged his head. "Poor dumb, love-struck bastard. I mean that in a good way." He swirled the coffee in his mug, his expression changing from something almost affectionate to a thoughtful frown. "All these years I've never asked you…what was it like for you, growing up with Jule as a stepmother?" His mouth quirked ironically. "And me as a brother? That must have scared you off starting a family. At least a little."

The question caught Dean by surprise. Though they shared the same father, he and Fletcher had been born to vastly different mothers. Victor Kingsley had married twice in his life—first Dean's mother, by all accounts a gentle and gracious woman who had died from cancer when Dean was only five, and then Jule, a far more flamboyant, mercurial and, ultimately, troubled young woman.

"I thought the early years were good," Dean said carefully. "Until Jule's bipolar disorder got really out of hand, there were some happy times for all of us. But I've never blamed her, Fletch—or you—for the problems."

Fletcher nodded. "Well, thanks for that. The problems, though…the fights and the separations…they make you wonder whether you can do it differently, don't they? Victor wasn't the greatest role model when it came to open lines of communication. I've had nights when I've woken up in full panic, wondering if I can give my kids a decent childhood, wondering whether I even know what that looks like."

Perspiration that had zilch to do with physical activity covered Dean's brow. He had an abrupt urge to bolt, leaving the stall—and the conversation—unfinished.

"You seem to be doing a good job," he told his brother. "The boys are happy. And you're already your daughter's hero."

The cowboy who had once seemed impervious to a

vulnerable moment began to look slightly green. "Yeah, that's now. I just thank God for Claire. She straightens me out when I start to stress."

"Well, this is great. Two grown men panicked over relationships."

"You want to email Dr. Phil?"

"Nope."

Dean shook his head. He was so screwed. Smitten by a woman—utterly, thoroughly smitten—for the first time in his life. About to become a husband and, in a few months, a father. Beneath the fear, he was excited about all of it, yet he couldn't get to know Rosemary—or rely on her for support— because of this thing, this lie, hanging over them. In addition to his headache, he'd been nursing serious nausea all day and wondered if he was experiencing sympathetic morning sickness or simple guilt.

"I'm forfeiting the building. I have to. I can't explain this to Rosemary in a way that will make sense."

"You mean you can't explain it in a way that won't make her think she's marrying into a family of lunatics."

On even the worst days of his life, Dean had been able to calm his mind and his body, to keep his reactions sane and focused. Millie, who'd worked at King's since Dean was a kid, had once told him he would never need a blood-pressure pill. It appeared those days were gone; he felt as if the pressure in his body were going to pop his head off like a cork.

Smacking his fist again the stall, he said, "I need the kind of chance we'd have if this were a normal relationship."

"Kingsleys don't do normal."

"I do."

"You gave it the old college try," Fletcher agreed. "But you were alone. Try to do 'normal' now that you're alive below the neck."

Dean longed to take offense. Before Rosemary, he'd have

argued that his emotions were present, simply calm and sane, unlike Fletcher's. Now he knew better. Now he knew what passion was.

"I can't tell Rosemary about the will, not yet. I've started my family with more baggage than we can handle. I've got to get rid of the problem, and that means forfeiting the building."

Once the words were out, Dean felt a weight lift from his shoulders. "I'll talk to Doug and the rest of the city council, try to make them understand how necessary the clinic is for the underinsured. Maybe they'll do the right thing and donate the building for the clinic."

"Will you tell Alberto?"

The weight pressed down again, like a lead yoke. "I'll have to. But not until I speak to Gwen and the others. And look around for another venue if I have to. Alberto has the most riding on this." His stomach began to churn, and he wondered if love made that a continual state of affairs. "He's got to make sense of his daughter's death."

Fletcher's sober gaze skewered his brother. "And Rosemary? What's next?"

"That's easier," Dean said, praying he was right. "We get married. Fall in love and have a baby. In that order."

Dean and Rosemary sittin' in a tree. K-i-s-s-i-n-g. First comes marriage, then comes love, then comes Dean Jr. in a baby carriage....

Rosemary stared at the skinny platinum band that had joined her engagement ring four days ago, the singsongy lyrics of the old children's melody playing in her mind as she wondered what to wear. Dean would be home...home to her house...in half an hour.

She had dinner—chicken, shallot and baby portabello casserole in a sublime Burgundy sauce—bubbling in the oven. She'd set the table with multicolored braided tapers and the blown-glass stemware she'd purchased after regifting Vi with her wedding crystal. Three potential outfits were laid out on the bed, awaiting her decision. A lot had changed in four days.

She had married Dean in Reno on Saturday. They had "honeymooned" for a couple of days then returned to Honeyford last night. This evening he was going to begin the process of moving into her place.

Rosemary stood at the foot of her queen-size bed, trying to decide between jeans and a boat-necked pullover in powder blue or a more formal skirt and sweater combo, when the phone rang.

Checking the caller ID, she smiled. "Hi, Daph. I was going to try you tomorrow."

"That is way too late." Her friend's voice sounded muffled.

"Watcha doin'?" Rosemary asked, holding the blue sweater up and tilting her head at the mirror. "You sound funny."

"I'm eating coconut-milk ice cream," she said around an apparently large mouthful. "It's *sooooo* good. Have you ever tried it?"

"Which flavor?"

"Coffee chip for dinner. I had Almond Joy as a midafternoon snack—that was good, too—piña colada for lunch, and triple-fudge-brownie for breakfast. My commitment to celibacy is going really well."

Rosemary smiled. "Sounds like it."

"So how about you? You've been married four whole days…and nights. Are *you* still celibate?"

"Yes."

"Bummer." Daphne shoved another spoonful of coffee chip into her mouth. "How was the wedding?"

Rosemary returned the sweater to the bed and moved to her dresser to pluck a pair of turquoise drops from an earring tree. "It was nice. I thought we'd get married at city hall or next to a blackjack table, but Dean found a chapel that was actually kind of sweet. Pitched roof, white gingerbread trim, pansies out front…."

"Awwww. Were you married by a minister?"

"I don't know. He had teased hair and offered an Elvis option. Does that say *minister* to you?"

Daphne laughed. "From the church of Elvis, yes. Did Dean kiss you?"

"Um, chastely."

"Darn. What did you do after you got married?"

"Well—" Rosemary poked the earrings into her lobes "—as we left, the minister's wife tossed birdseed and then handed us a pamphlet of their services, which include but are not limited to shuttle service to and from local casinos, infant baptism and marriage-dissolution counseling should the need arise."

"Sounds like every girl's dream wedding."

"Yup. Once we were alone, there was a moment of, shall we say, extreme awkwardness outside the chapel. Then Dean kissed my hand and said, 'Thank you for marrying me. Let's go somewhere else for the infant baptism.'"

Daphne laughed. "I like your husband."

Happy bubbles, reminiscent of the champagne she hadn't been able to drink, floated up from Rosemary's stomach. "I like him, too," she whispered, so softly she wasn't sure her friend heard until Daphne whooped.

"Details, please!"

Rosemary smiled. She and Dean had "honeymooned," otherwise known as Making the Marriage Look Real, by driving to Virginia City, where they had shopped, played slot machines (Rosemary won forty dollars on an old-fashioned nickel machine) and ate excellent chili at a little hole-in-the-wall. They returned to Reno at night, went to their—*separate*—

rooms, changed and attended a performance of Cirque du Soleil. And they talked.

They talked about Dean's college days and hers, about their favorite childhood hobbies (bug collection and tennis for him; cooking in her Easy-Bake Oven and ice skating for her), and about child-rearing philosophies (they had both purchased Patrice Moore's *Back to Basics* and loved the common-sense approach).

Every night, Dean walked Rosemary to her hotel room, held her hand, kissed her cheek and said, "Thank you."

Every night, she imagined how it would feel if he stayed.

When she admitted that out loud, Daphne's voice filled with wonder. "Honestly? You're falling for him?"

Rosemary closed her eyes. "I'm weak. Tell me I'm weak and that I'm conducting my life like a romantic comedy and that carpe diem dating is the only good idea I've had since I bought the Barbie-and-Ken wedding suite."

"Carpe diem dating is a really good idea," Daphne said dutifully, "in theory. In reality, it's kind of like crocheting a zip line. You can try and try, but it's never gonna hold. We're die-hard romantics, Rosemary."

"But you're committed to celibacy. That's a plan to keep from being hurt again. It's okay not to want to be hurt, right?"

On the other end of the line, Daphne sighed. "Well, I'm still planning to date, so I'll probably still get hurt. I'm just trying to weed out the real contenders from the phonies."

"Which makes excellent sense!"

"Yes. For me. But, Rosemary, what if you've already found your real contender? What if Dean Kingsley is your destiny, and you keep resisting until it's time for you to split up and then it's too late?"

Rosemary felt hiccups coming on. "If Dean Kingsley were

my destiny, I would know for certain, wouldn't I? I mean, I would be feeling peace right now."

"I don't know. Destiny could be like coconut ice cream. You'll never know how right it's going to be unless you dive in and take a bite. Then…kismet."

"Kismet," Rosemary murmured.

"One more thing you might want to consider," Daphne said, and Rosemary could tell she was enjoying the ice cream again. "This whole celibacy thing?"

"Yeah?"

"It's really fattening."

Dean arrived bearing a suitcase and a gift for his bride.

"Crystallized ginger," he announced, handing her a package of cellophane-wrapped candy. "My sister-in-law swears there's nothing better for morning sickness. If it works, we'll start carrying it at the drugstore. And these—" he whipped a bouquet of two dozen long-stemmed yellow roses out from beneath his arm and lowered his voice to the intimate caress that sent goose bumps racing down her arms "—are for the beautiful lady of the house."

"Thank you." Rosemary accepted both gifts, leading the way into her cottage-style home. Nerves rattled her bones. Dean always managed to appear utterly sincere when he said things that made him sound as if he'd walked out of a Frank Capra movie. In fact, he *looked* as if he'd walked out of a Frank Capra movie.

His chestnut hair was thick as turf; his jaw looked as if a master sculptor had formed it. Broad shoulders, a flat stomach and a perpetual smile in eyes as blue as a Honeyford summer sky could make any woman feel good about being alive. But with Dean, Rosemary often got the feeling that his sole purpose was to make *her* feel good.

Smiling shyly over her shoulder, she caught sight of his suitcase—evidence that he truly was moving into her home.

They had discussed it, of course, while in Reno, and both agreed that moving into her larger two-bedroom cottage made the most sense over the next couple of years. Still, her heart thumped heavily at the prospect. She had never lived with anyone other than her family and ex-husband. Leading Dean through the living room, she paused in the small square hallway that opened onto the downstairs bedroom, the stair-well leading to the upper floor and the sole bathroom in the house.

"You remember those girls in college who were completely comfortable living in coed dorms and diving into swimming pools in their underwear at parties?" she asked.

Bemused, Dean nodded. "Uh, yeah. I do."

Rosemary broke the sad news. "I wasn't one of them." She opened the glass door that closed the attic bedroom off from the rest of the house. "I'm putting you upstairs. I moved my things down here so I can use the bathroom and kitchen a little more easily once my pregnancy progresses. Since I'm an early riser, I thought I'd take my shower first in the morning. Or, we can talk about it. It's actually a claw-foot tub with a shower attachment… I hope that's okay."

He nodded.

"I usually start a pot of coffee first thing, too. You're wel-come to share if you're a coffee drinker in the morning."

Another nod.

"All right." She wished for a little more from him. Making plans was very calming. Why did men not get that? "Well. Then generally I take a walk—I pack my breakfast and bring it along—and I wind up at work."

Dean mulled over what she was telling him, but made no comment other than a noncommittal, "Ah."

"When the baby comes," Rosemary persisted, certain her

tension would subside once all strategies, present and future, were neatly laid out, "I can have the crib in my room. All the floors are hardwood with the exception of the upstairs bedroom, but when the baby starts serious crawling I'll go rug shopping for something soft on the knees. And we might need to replace this glass door." She tapped it. "A solid wood panel would be much safer. Or we could use a baby gate down here and install a door to the bedroom upstairs for privacy. What do you think?"

He smiled gently. "I think you're an intelligent, conscientious woman who is understandably ambivalent about having a roommate she didn't anticipate. Now you've got the next two years planned out down to the minute. You're remarkable. But I find that where you're concerned, Rosemary Josephine, I've got my hands full just taking it one night at a time."

From someone else that could have been a put-down, but Dean wasn't telling her not to plan, just saying he needed to evaluate things in the moment. Rosemary realized he possessed the quality of stillness. Even on that first night, as he'd flirted with her, there had been something steady and unshakable about him. It wasn't that he hadn't cared about the outcome, but rather that he trusted the outcome to be okay, whatever it was.

"Wow," she whispered, "that was *such* a nice way of saying I'm uptight."

He leaned toward her, or maybe she was imagining it, because *she* wanted to be several inches closer. "I like you uptight. Gives me an excuse to try to relax you."

Rosemary licked her dry lips. "Do you have a *plan* to accomplish that?"

The smile in his eyes expanded to a grin. "Why, yes, Rosemary. As a matter of fact, I do." He raised his suitcase. "I'll show myself upstairs and put this away. Meet me back here in fifteen minutes."

She laughed at the notion of specifying a place to "meet." The entire first floor of her cottage occupied eight hundred square feet. "Okay, fifteen minutes."

Rosemary watched him head upstairs, easygoing, relaxed, taking this next step in his life with enviable calm.

I hope the baby has his personality.

Her breath pinched in her chest. It was the first time she'd thought about whom the baby would take after or whom she hoped the baby would take after.

Placing a hand on her stomach, she felt a near-overwhelming urge to follow Dean upstairs and show him the little mound of her belly.

Here, she would say, *feel. That's her, little Montana Jeffers Kingsley.* And Dean would laugh and argue lightly. *You mean little Nate Jeffers Kingsley.* Then he would put his warm, gentle hand on her stomach, and his expression would change, assuming the serious, contemplative air she was coming to know. Their eyes would meet, the pressure of his hand would increase a bit, and she'd see again what she'd noticed several times already but had deliberately glossed over—desire. The hunger he had to touch her bare skin, to possess the woman who carried his child.

As if her feet had brains, they danced with the yearning to race him to the attic. And the queen-size bed. Would the sex be as good now as it had been that first night?

Gritting her teeth, she pivoted from the stairs, marched herself to the kitchen and grabbed a vase for the roses. Before she attended to the flowers, however, she turned on the faucet and stuck her arms beneath the stream of water, giving herself the cold shower she so desperately needed.

"Ohhhh," Rosemary groaned. "Mmm...amazing. I'm so glad I married you."

Dean laughed. "Stick with me, baby. I've got connections."

He forked up another piece of the Double Trouble Chocolate Pie his sister-in-law, Claire, had baked for them.

After he'd come back downstairs, he'd handed Rosemary a DVD then went out to the car he'd parked in the gravel alongside her front yard and returned with the pink bakery box wrapped in string.

They'd watched the first half of *The Music Man*. "Featuring," Dean had said, explaining his movie selection, "Marion the Librarian, in honor of the most beautiful librarian I know." He'd kissed the tip of her nose.

They'd sat a thigh's width apart on her green velour couch while Professor Harold Hill played his con game and wooed the übercautious librarian. When Marion sang "Goodnight, My Someone" to the soul mate she believed she might never find, Rosemary burst into wet blubbers, feeling as mature as a nine-month-old, and causing Dean to scoot over and put his arm around her. That arm had felt perfect, and she'd cried some more until he'd tipped her face up to his, wiped the tears and looked as if he was going to kiss her.

She'd waited, lips parted, hoping the leaky-nose issue was all taken care of, because she was so going to kiss him back. With the snuffling past, her libido went on the rampage *again* (horny pregnant women were obviously no old wives' tale), and she waited for him to make the move.

Which turned out not to be a kiss.

He'd clicked off the movie, called "Intermission" and stood up to cut the pie.

Damn good thing it had two layers of fudge and a rich cookie crust, because extra shots of chocolate were the only way she was going to medicate her sexual frustration tonight.

She honestly couldn't remember feeling sexually frustrated before. Ever. Dissatisfied, yeah, but climb-out-of-my-skin, gotta-jump-your-bones, don't-talk-just-do-it-to-me-now frustrated? Uh-uh.

"This should be made an illegal substance," Rosemary said, licking the back of her fork. "I'll drop by the bakery before work tomorrow and thank Claire in person."

"She'd love to see you, I'm sure."

Tilting her head back against the sofa, Rosemary sighed. "Daphne was right. Celibacy is fattening."

Vaguely surprised she'd said that out loud, she glanced at Dean, who had taken a sip of the decaf they'd made and now struggled not to spit it out. Once he'd swallowed, he said, "Daphne the cute blonde is celibate?"

Rosemary nodded. "Although I'm not sure I should have said anything. It's probably too much information."

Dean wagged his head. "Len is going to be very disappointed. He's been all over me to get her phone number from you."

"Don't tell him," Rosemary insisted, though she didn't think Daphne kept her celibacy a secret. In fact, quite the contrary when it came to men, since she currently viewed the willingness to wait as something of a test. "Why is sex so important to men, anyway?" Rosemary wondered aloud.

"To men?" Dean's mouth twitched. "It's important to women, too, isn't it?"

He was amused, which made Rosemary feel about forty years older than she was and not very sexy. She'd brought it on herself, of course, and considered dropping the subject altogether, but she was slightly drunk on sugar and for much of her sexually active life she had honestly wondered what the big deal was.

"What I mean is, making love can be...fun. But sex changes, like everything else in a relationship. I suppose it's never been that important to me."

"Why not?"

She shrugged.

"Describe sex in one word. An adjective," he challenged.

"I can't—"

"I bet you have a bachelor's degree in English," he guessed. She did. "Give me a word."

"Well, it's…nice."

He set his plate on the coffee table. "'Nice?' Rosie Jo," he said, his voice a velvet lion's purr, "are you saying what we did at the motel was only 'nice'?"

If she were a match, she'd be lit now. "No. That was more… that was…um…"

"Yes?"

"More than nice."

Blue sparks of humor and challenge shot from his eyes. He seemed half amused, half disgusted when he shook his head. "Nope. You're a librarian. Pick an *accurate* adjective to describe you, me and that king-size bed."

Rosemary tried to swallow, but there was nothin' doin'. Her throat had frozen up on her. She croaked out a weak, "Well…" then cleared her throat and started to perspire. "What would you call it?"

His eyes narrowed, his gaze locked on her. "Astonishing. Inimitable. Transforming. Scorching."

Oh. Scorching. Good adjective. Yes, definitely scorching….

Do not confuse sex with love. Do not confuse sex with love. Do not confuse sex with love.

Rosemary recalled the eleventh commandment in her mother's home, imparted with all the gravitas of Moses on the Mount.

"All I meant," she said, speaking slowly and laboriously since she didn't have a drop of spit left in her mouth, "when we started this conversation was that if Len is serious about getting to know Daphne, then he shouldn't care whether she's fully clothed or bottoms-up naked. That's all."

Dean looked at her. A long time. Finally he said, "With all the books in that library of yours, there's got to be one that explains the natural science of man and woman."

Rosemary bristled at the implication that she didn't have a grasp on male-female relationships. Which, okay, she didn't. Even though she'd been married ten years, and that made the situation especially sad. But she did know about lust. She knew that it could start a relationship and that it could end one. What it could not do was make a relationship last.

"I understand physical desire," she insisted. "I know that lust can start a relationship. It can also end one. But it can't make a relationship last, which is why focusing on personality is important."

"Personality is job one," he agreed easily. Putting his elbow on the back of the couch he leaned against one bent knuckle and regarded her at length. "The thing is, if I had you naked, with that dark, curly hair falling around your shoulders—" he was back to the low, velvet voice that gave her shivers "—and those big cat eyes staring up at me, and if you were willing, I would not be concentrating on your character traits, as much as I admire them." He reached out to loop one of the loose curls around his finger. "I'd be taking the opportunity to get to know you intimately…very intimately…and most definitely involving every part of that gorgeous body. More than once. So—" he continued to play idly with her hair, and Rosemary felt the combustion from the desire building inside her "—your friend Daphne is probably right. If she wants Len, or any man, to know her mind and heart first, then celibacy is a good idea."

All the while he talked about celibacy, he caressed Rosemary with his eyes and toyed with her hair, winding the curls around his fingers until he reached her jawline. Then he burrowed his fingers through the thick brown strands be-hind her ear and at her nape. His palm cupped the back of her head.

Rosemary's vision began to blur. *Hang on, Rosemary, hang on,* she encouraged herself, but deep down she feared she was about to become fodder for The Learning Channel: *Internal Combustion—Real or an Urban Legend?* He looked at her as if she was already naked. *Damn it, kiss me already.* They were going to set the city on fire.

She leaned forward. He did, too.

"Fortunately," he said, "I'm already in touch with your per-sonality. So if you're really, *really* concerned about celibacy being fattening..."

"I am," Rosemary breathed, "I *really* am."

Dean smiled. "Well, then I'm going to help. I refuse to allow my wife to worry unnecessarily."

He tugged her all the way toward him, and Rosemary went. Willingly.

Chapter Twelve

"You did it. You did the naughty bump with the pharmacist."

"Vi, for heaven's sake—"

"You did. I can hear it in the way you say his name. 'Dean,'" she sighed, her voice high and breathy.

"I don't sound like that. I've never in my life—"

"Was it recreational sex or are you hoping this marriage is going to go live?" She didn't let more than a couple of seconds elapse. "Oh, my God, you're hoping. So much for carpe diem dating."

Rosemary considered knocking herself unconscious against a bookshelf in the Travel aisle. The library was going to open in ten minutes. She shouldn't be having a conversation about this now, but Daphne had phoned Vi to give her the details on the wedding, and Vi had called Rosemary to heckle her and to ask whether there was going to be a reception.

There was, at the Honeyford Community Center, in one

week's time. Both she and Dean had tried to talk his...their... sister-in-law, Claire, out of planning the party, but she had a cadre of townspeople working with her, and they wouldn't take no for an answer. Moreover they wanted to stage this shindig soon, because the Honeyford Days spring celebration was coming up in late April, and the community center would be unavailable.

Rosemary's first wedding reception had taken place at the Governor Hotel in downtown Portland. She'd had a wedding planner, a caterer, several other people on cell phones orchestrating the entire thing, plus Vi, Daphne and Ginger running interference between Rosemary and her weddingphobic family.

"Daphne says Dean wants a real marriage, open-ended," Vi said, her voice subdued for her. "Do you think this guy is the real deal?"

It was an unusual question for Vi. As long as Rosemary had known her tough, independent friend, Via Lynn Harris had assumed that no man was the real deal regarding love and fidelity.

Pressing *Fodor's Italy* neatly on the shelf so its spine aligned with the other titles, Rosemary closed her eyes, allowing mental images from the past two days to shimmer tantalizingly behind her closed lids....

She and Dean making love, with tenderness and with abandon, with humor and with utter earnestness. Appropriate adjectives? Stupendous, staggering, indescribable, astonishing.

The non-naked hours had been just as good. Better, because those were the hours that were making her a believer again.

Dean had discussed parenting philosophies with interest and opinions. He was, he told her, going to be front-row-center for all ball games and dance recitals.

"What if we have an introverted child who isn't into sports teams or performing? she had asked.

He'd given that some thought. "We'll start Team Kingsley with his cousins. No pressure. Pure fun and physical fitness."

"What if *she* doesn't want to be in a dance recital?"

"Every kid likes to perform for her family. Fletcher and I will build a stage on the ranch. She and Rozzy can put on plays. I'll hang the out-to-lunch sign and run over for a noon performance."

He would, too.

Rosemary had stared at his gorgeous, smiling, gonna-be-the-proudest-pop-on-the-block expression, and…oh, good golly. *Help, I've fallen and I can't get up.*

They hadn't talked only about children, either. In fact, up to that point he had spoken directly to her tummy only once, a quick, "Hellooo. How's the view in there? Everything is A-OK up here."

Hanging around the house in the evening, they had discovered a shared fondness for Shakespeare and had both seen the Oregon Shakespeare Festival's production of *Much Ado About Nothing,* which they'd happily dissected. Oddly, they had both chosen the actor in the smaller role of The Friar as their favorite performer. "He had a great grasp on the language without seeming stiff or less human," Dean had said.

"Hmm." Rosemary had thought back to what made the actor so appealing to her at the time. Daphne and Ginger had wanted to wait outside after the show to get his autograph. "He seemed to truly care about Hero. And I loved the way he calmed everyone down and told them how to fix the mess they were all in." *Just the way you would.* "He seemed like the kind of guy you'd want around during a natural disaster. And that voice! When he took charge…" She'd shivered conspicuously. "Quite a looker, too, as I recall." She'd peeked at Dean mock shyly as she'd washed a bowl in the kitchen sink. "Daphne and Ginger were crushing."

Dean had narrowed his gaze. Under her guidance, he'd been rolling chocolate-chip cookie dough into balls and setting them on a baking sheet. He'd been quite dutiful about it, too, eating only every other dough ball, but now left his post to advance on her with exaggerated gravity. "And you, Mrs. Kingsley? Were you 'crushing,' too, or is your interest strictly thespian?"

"Oh, my interest is arts-related, for sure." She'd nodded broadly. "And he was some work of art. I wonder if he lives in Oregon? I could invite him over—"

"That does it." Dean had grabbed her round the waist, burying his mouth against her neck and nuzzling the spot that gave her goose bumps from head to toe. "The next play you go to is *The Trojan Women*."

Grinning, Rosemary had turned her head until their lips met. Dean hesitated not a second before kissing her more deeply than he ever had. Soon she had turned against his chest, and they were clinging to each other—arms, lips, legs tangling. Rosemary's bones had melted on the spot as she'd realized she loved everything she knew about the man: the way he spoke to people—so focused and considerate; the myriad collection jars he displayed on his counter at work and the fact that he helped fill them up every night; his kindness toward Honeyford's elderly population; and his humor.

She also liked the way he glanced over to see if she was looking before he popped more cookie dough into his mouth; the lingering looks at her bottom (one of her better features if she did say so herself) and then the grin and raised brows when she caught him.

She loved the way he smelled, too, the pure physical yumminess of the man. Every pore of her body opened to let him in, and she didn't want to—she couldn't—stop it.

Kissing him back with no reservation was like turning a key in the ignition of a race car that had been waiting for the chance to go from zero to a hundred. Dean roared to life. He'd kissed her back with a hunger that sucked her onto the speedway with him. All she could do, all she wanted to do, was hang on for the ride.

She wasn't sure how long they'd stood in the kitchen, wrapped in and around each other, but when he'd picked her up and headed out of the room, she was more than ready. Their lips had connected the entire way with Dean muttering between kisses, "No actor playing a friar is going to make love to you the way I'm going to."

Rosemary had grinned, kissing him hungrily until he practically sprinted up the stairs. Never had a discussion about classical theatre been more gratifying.

"Hey, you there?" Vi prodded.

"I'm here." Rosemary opened her eyes and straightened away from the shelf she'd been leaning against. She checked the clock above periodicals. Two minutes to opening time. Dean had developed a habit of dropping by for lunch. She couldn't wait.

"Vi, I'm going to tell you something, but don't respond with anything sarcastic or even teasing, okay? I'm very sensitive lately." She took a deep breath. "Here's the thing—I think I've been given my second chance at the picket fence. Dean seems like that too-good-to-be-true guy, except that he's also authentic and dependable. He loves kids, and he's so good with them, Vi. And I know it's too early to be sure, but he doesn't seem like the kind of man who would play around. He has integrity."

"How is he in the sack? Wait, scratch that. Insensitive." Vi sighed heavily. "Okay, I'm glad it's happening for you. And I'm not being sarcastic. The whole 'happily ever after' thing… I guess I just stopped buying into it. But if you believe it, I'm on board."

Rosemary could see Mrs. Spinelli-Adamson waiting at

the door with her customary shopping bag full of books to return. She cradled the phone and spoke softly. "Vi, that year you spent studying in Rome…we all knew there was a special guy, but you've never said why you broke up other than that he didn't want to move to America. When are you going to tell us what really happened?"

There was a brief silence then a too-brittle laugh. "When pizzas fly, *cara*." Before Rosemary could say anything else, Vi said briskly, "So what's the 411 on your reception? Daphne, Ginger and I are driving down together."

"Oh, my gosh, no. Don't—I mean, really do not—come all the way out here for this thing. It's just a little get-together at the community center. My sister-in-law had to book it between Friday night bingo and a Sunday meeting of the Honeyford Succulents Garden Club. We'll probably have a cactus on every table. Don't come. I'd rather keep things low-key and very, very brief."

Vi made a rude buzzer sound. "Uh-uh. You're having a wedding reception, and you think your three best friends in the world aren't going to come? Especially when *I* was the one who encouraged you to sleep—I mean, dance—with the man in the first place? Guess again, little mama-to-be. Now, you tell me the when and where of this shindig, and we'll make it a party befitting the potential last husband you're ever going to need."

Claire had promised Dean and Rosemary a "simple," "low-key," "modest" wedding reception.

"Don't even think of it as a reception, then," she had urged when Rosemary begged her to keep it small. "Think of it as a welcome-to-the-neighborhood party, just an opportunity for people to stop in and say hi and acknowledge that you're a couple now. Not a big deal."

So Rosemary envisioned the multipurpose room of the

Honeyford Community Center dotted with a few balloons, a bouquet of spring flowers from Geri Evans's garden, a portable CD player—perhaps with "Because You Loved Me" on repeat mode—a cake from Honey Bea's and some punch. Maybe thirty people with nothing better to do on a Saturday evening would show up at the community center.

Low-key. Where she and Dean and their so-new relationship would not be held up to scrutiny.

"I'm not going in," she said stubbornly, ducking behind a large planter of Cordyline as she peered in horror at the festivities inside. Twinkle lights festooned the room. Irene Gould walked by in a floor-length gold lamé skirt, hauling Henry Berns, the baker, along with her toward a makeshift dance floor. A crystal ball rotated slowly overhead while a live band—not Celine Dion via boom box but a *live* band for pity's sake—played Faith Hill's "This Kiss." A fountain of punch graced the center of a table bearing the weight of chafing dishes and platters of hors d'oeuvres.

"This is no good!" Rosemary hissed at Dean from her spot behind the plant. "I'm getting fatter by the second! We were supposed to let a few people guess the truth and then spread it around town while we look the other way." She gestured angrily toward the door. "Half the town is in there right now!"

Standing with his hands in his pockets, lips compressed and eyebrows raised, Dean obligingly glanced inside the noisy room. "Nah. The community center can't hold half the town. And it's against the fire marshal's rules. There's probably no more than…one third in there." He sniffed the air, redolent with the aroma of food. "I smell Josef's cabbage rolls. The Honeyford Inn must have catered. Let's go." Rosemary groaned, which elicited a sympathetic smile from her husband. "Did you bring your ginger?"

"I'm not worried about that!"

He approached the planter. "Rosie—"

"Go away. I'm not coming out. Tell them I have the flu."

"Again? That's what we told everyone the night I proposed. And didn't you tell everyone at the library you had the flu when you threw up?"

"All right, all right! Then say I caught a terrible cold." She coughed as an example of "terrible." "You go in. It's dark. I'll stay close to the bushes and run on home."

Dean grabbed her as she commenced her great escape and pulled her in for a hug, stroking her hair with the soothing touch that made her feel immensely comforted. "You're only showing a little, Rosie Jo." When she began to protest, he cut her off. "It looks like a lot to us, because we're excited about the baby." In fact they had spent much of last night looking at the bump from all angles in the mirror after a steamy, sexy shower. "But to the people in there, that tiny mound could look like nothing more than too many of Claire's Honey Bunz."

He nuzzled behind her ear, and Claire melted against him. She was so easy. "I just don't want to be asked a lot of questions that have private answers."

"Stick with me kid. I won't let the paparazzi get you down."

Claire smiled against his lapel and socked him lightly in the ribs. "Fine. I'm making too big a deal of it. I plead the hormone defense."

"Plead any defense you want." He kissed her long and deep then murmured, "Let's get this over with so we can go home."

Putty to his sculptor's hands, Rosemary followed without another word. Going home at night had become her favorite part of the day. Sometimes she beat him to the cottage and made dinner; sometimes he arrived home first and had her favorite mac and cheese waiting for her. But almost always before they ate, they satisfied the other, stronger hungers that had built up during the hours apart. Though his baby grew inside her, they were newlyweds experiencing all the excitement and wonder of setting up house.

"There they are!" Someone—Rosemary couldn't identify the voice—shouted above the music to draw the crowd's attention to the door as she and Dean walked in.

"This Kiss" changed to a surprisingly sincere rendition of The Captain & Tenille's "Muskrat Love," with the band, Honeyford's own Crystallized Honey, a group of sixtysomething musicians who had come out of retirement for Dean's brother's wedding, altering the lyrics to "Muskrat Rosemary, Muskrat Dean, do the jitterbug in their muskrat dreams..."

Dozens of people flocked to the door, shaking Dean's hand, hugging Rosemary and telling her how thrilled they were that one of the town's favorite sons had finally found his bride.

"Love couldn't happen to a more deserving man," Dolores Schenk sighed, holding Rosemary's arm in a grip made tight partly from emotion and partly because the nonagenarian refused to use her walker. "He gives me all my medications at cost, bless his heart. I've prayed every day that he would find himself a good woman. And now he has. A librarian." She waxed eloquently about the importance of education for a woman until her great-granddaughter eased her away.

Rosemary didn't see much of Dean for an hour as the confidences and back slapping continued. The party was in full swing when Vi, Daphne and Ginger swept through the community center's double doors. They found Rosemary immediately and spirited her away from her library clerk, Abby, who had dressed in a black lace Victorian ensemble reflecting her current reading material—*Tess of the d'Urbervilles*—and Abby's boyfriend, Colin, who wore black leather jeans and bore a striking resemblance to Johnny Depp in *Edward Scissorhands*.

"Great band," Vi yelled above the noise. "Haven't I seen them on *The Lawrence Welk Show?*"

"Shh." Rosemary shook her head at her friend. "Apparently they came out of retirement for my brother-in-law's wedding and now they're unstoppable."

"Speaking of your hottie brother-in-law." Vi grinned wickedly, her red lips parting to reveal even teeth that had obviously undergone another round of laser whitening. "Where is he? I need a photo so I can lord it over my Pilates class—I stood next to the Tuff Enuff jeans butt."

Rosemary gazed at her three best friends and broke out in a huge, tear-filled smile. "I'm so glad you're here." They shared a group hug. "I've been ridiculously nervous about tonight."

"Aw, why, sweetie?" Daphne, who wore a powder-blue knit dress that made her look like a Victoria's Secret angel but with more clothes, slipped a comforting arm around Rosemary's waist. "You look wonderful. Refreshed and happy."

"Do I?" Rosemary sniffed, accepting a tissue from Ginger as she tried to stem the waterworks.

Ginger nodded. "You do. You were meant for marriage and motherhood, honey. And it appears you and your man are well-loved." She glanced around. "There's a lot of support in this room. Isn't this everything you wanted?"

Those words—*everything you wanted*—felt like ice cubes bobbing in Rosemary's blood. No, this wasn't everything she'd ever wanted. It was more.

She'd dreamt of the man and the children, but now she had an entire community around her, too. Every day the library became more and more her home away from home. She had started a book club and a Read to the Dogs program. When she went to the bank, the tellers greeted her by name, and yesterday Jan Tuma, the owner of Yellow Jacket Gently Used Clothes, had rushed from her store when Rosemary walked past, eager to tell the librarian that her son, Alex, who previously had thought he was a poor reader, just finished the entire *A Wrinkle in Time* trilogy Rosemary had suggested.

She belonged.

And it all felt *sooooo* good that it frightened her. Losing her dreams the first time, with Neil, had been hard. She'd been in a scary depression for months after the divorce. If she fell for Once Upon a Time again and lost it when she was this close, lost Dean and the family she'd dreamed about since she was a child, she didn't know how she'd survive. And she had to, because now her—*their*—child was involved.

"Family-of-origin alert. Mother and sisters heading through the doors." Vi nodded toward the group that entered the Honeyford Community Center.

As Rosemary looked over her shoulder, her friends stepped closer, circling the wagons around her.

Rosemary's heart rate approached panic mode as her mother and sisters hovered on the threshold of the large multipurpose room, collectively looking like three earthling tourists who had been dropped off against their will on Mars.

Dressed in a Carolina Herrara suit that probably cost more than Rosemary's mortgage, and flanked by two of her daughters garbed in their own designer ensembles, Maeve Jeffers gazed at the small-town festivities—the twinkle lights, the Congratulations, Rosemary and Dean banner decorated in poster paints, the shiny ivory and white balloons, and the flowers stuffed in any vase that would have them, and you could tell she was sure she'd died and gone to Purgatory.

"Oh, holy heaven, I begged Lucy not to say anything about tonight." Rosemary's gaze jerked around the room.

"Are you looking for Dean?" Daphne put a hand out to steady her friend.

"No. I'm looking for an escape route."

"Rosemary, you cannot leave your groom alone with new in-laws." Vi wagged a finger whose red-painted nail bore a skull-and-crossbones tattoo. "Especially *his* new in-laws.

Ginger, you help Rosemary find Dean. Daphne and I will handle Medea and the Greek Chorus. Come on, Daph."

Only Daphne could make nausea look sexy. "Nothin' doin'. It's nothing personal, Rosemary, but Maeve scares me."

Vi rolled her eyes, but reassigned the jobs, pulling Ginger along and shooing Daphne and Rosemary away.

They located Dean standing near the refreshments table, speaking to a thirtysomething woman who looked like Holly Hobbie come to life. Rather than the striking bottle-red locks that Vi sported so well, this woman's naturally curly hair was Opie-orange, thick and gorgeously unruly, a perfect complement to the amber freckles that dusted her milk-white skin. Gi-normous blue-gray eyes claimed most of the real estate on her face, leaving room for a small, rounded nose and puffy, cupid's-bow lips. Viewed individually, her features were quirky, but they worked in harmony to create a face one could look at a long time and not tire of.

Dean was nodding and smiling as they spoke.

"Wow, this is the first time I've seen your man since December," Daphne said as she and Rosemary approached, arm in arm. "He's even hunkier than I remembered. Who's the woman?"

"I don't know her name, but I understand she owns the barbershop on Main Street. I've seen her through the window a few times."

"The barbershop?" Daphne's energy picked up. "She's around men all day? Is she married?"

"I don't know." Rosemary frowned at her friend's tone. "Why?"

"If she's around men for hours at a time, she ought to be comfortable with them, but she's nervous as a cat with Dean. Watch her. Keeps pushing her hair behind her ears, nervous smile. Major crush there."

After several days without morning sickness, Rosemary began to feel ill.

"You have nothing to worry about, though," Daphne assured her.

"How can you tell?"

Daphne stopped walking and looked at her friend in fond amazement. "Honestly, Rosemary, you're such a babe in the woods sometimes. Dean has no idea that woman is the slightest bit interested. Look at his eyes and his smile—extremely polite. One-hundred-percent platonic. He's oblivious. Which is very sweet where you're concerned, but übersad for her. I wonder how long she's been carrying a torch?"

Rosemary marveled at her friend's boy-girl acumen. Indeed, as they closed in on the chatting duo and Dean looked up to see his wife's approach, his expression transformed completely. The well-mannered attention he showed the redhead clicked into an expression that was keenly alert and pheromone-soaked. His eyes smiled, physical tension tightened his body and his lips broadened in a grin that was all for his wife. He didn't even glance at Daphne, who, Rosemary figured, was sexier than she could hope to be in this or three more lifetimes.

Her blood sang, the attraction one-hundred-percent mutual.

He's mine. The sense of connectedness that had gone missing for the past few years was back, and now she yearned for more. *I want Dean Kingsley to be my best friend.* The thought stopped her in her tracks. She wanted all the things Dean talked about when he proposed.

Beside her, Daphne squeezed her arm. "Rosemary Jeffers Kingsley," she whispered with a smile in her voice, "get a room."

"Tried that," Rosemary whispered back, her gaze on Dean. "That's why we're here."

When they reached Dean, he introduced Gabriella Coombs, owner/operator of Honey Comb's barbershop, and Rosemary reintroduced him to Daphne, but their eyes never strayed long from each other.

"Congratulations, Rosemary," Gabriella said, sweetly and politely. Rosemary shifted her focus from Dean to his friend long enough to see the pain that clouded her rainy-day eyes. "I hope you're enjoying H-Honeyford."

Oh, sweet baby Jane, she's going to cry. Daphne was right: the barber was in love with Dean.

Compassion, not jealousy or fear, filled Rosemary. She gave the woman a smile. "Thank you. It's a wonderful town. I hope…I hope we'll get to know each other better, Gabby."

With a brave nod and a last, sad glance at Dean, Gabby excused herself.

Daphne began to chat about the party, engaging Dean, who slipped an arm around his wife's waist, while Rosemary collected herself. Gabby Coombs's loneliness was a palpable thing, and Rosemary knew that if it hadn't been for one aberrant night in December, she would be looking at a future far, far different from the one that currently opened before her.

She studied Dean as he spoke animatedly about small business with Daphne.

Two years of marriage will never be enough. Dean's hand made gentle up and down strokes along Rosemary's expanding waist. Last night he'd treated her to a full body massage, placing his palm protectively over her stomach and whispering in Rosemary's ear, "Ours."

She had waited all her life, it seemed, to feel like this, like part of something sweet and strong and timeless as the sea—a family. Because she had stopped expecting it to happen, she'd almost missed it. Dean had sneaked up on her, moving staunchly through her fears like a soldier marching through a sandstorm.

Thank you, she thought. *Oh, my God, thank you for not giving up.*

"What do you think, Rosemary? Yoo-hoo. Rosemary!"

Hearing her name after it had been called a couple of times, Rosemary blinked. "What?"

Daphne gave them her angel's grin. "I said the food smells great, but something tells me that's not what's on *your* mind." She nudged Dean. "Dance with your wife. I think she'll be putty in your arms."

He grinned. "Try the pierogis," he said to Daphne as she strolled away, then leaned down to nuzzle his wife's neck. "And I'll try you."

Crystallized Honey began "My Eyes Adored You" as Dean and Rosemary took to the floor. The silly crystal ball spun slowly above them; the balloons bobbed as children played with their strings; the twinkle lights looked cheap, but charming as heck. Dean looped his hands at the small of his wife's back while she circled her arms around his neck. There was nowhere on earth she would rather be.

"Thank you for going along with this," Dean murmured as they swayed. "In Honeyford, the longtime residents tend to think of each other more as family than neighbors. They figure it's their right to throw us a reception."

"I'm glad they did," she said, meaning it. "I'm sorry I made such a fuss earlier. I can see I'm going to have to get used to a lot of community involvement if I'm going to be married to Honeyford's favorite son."

Dean laughed. "I am not their favorite son."

"You're definitely in the top five."

They grinned at each other. The urge to say more made Rosemary's heart thump with nerves.

Do it. You've been making love with the man, for heaven's sake. His baby is growing inside you. Tell him how you feel.

Like a softly running stream, their gazes flowed in the space between them. It felt so easy, this moment of intimate connection on a crowded dance floor…except for the confession that hovered on Rosemary's tongue.

As he often seemed to, Dean paved her way. "How about for you?" he questioned softly. "Have I made it to your top five yet?"

Chapter Thirteen

The pulse in Rosemary's throat shimmied. She shook her head. "Not the top five, no. I'd say…" Heat filled her face. *Take the plunge, Rosemary. Take the plunge.* "I'd say—"

Hic!

Not again! She hadn't hiccuped once since she'd said, "I do."

Hic!

Oh, for the love of heaven.

Leaning back a few inches, Dean watched his bride with wry acceptance. "You want some water?"

"No!" *Hic.* She pulled her arms from around his neck and slapped her chest in disgust. "This is so ridiculous."

Releasing his dance hold, Dean brought his hands up to cradle her face. "It's all right. I've learned to speak hiccup where you're concerned. You get them every time you're about to take a step toward me, did you know that? I have a theory."

Rosemary fell into his eyes. How could any man be so patient? So calm and so strong at the same time? "What is it?"

"Part of you wants to dive into the rabbit hole with me, but there's another part that wants to stay right where you are. The closer you get to jumping, the more tense you get, and—hiccups."

Rosemary frowned. "Rabbit hole? You're saying our relationship is like the rabbit hole in *Alice in Wonderland?* That's not very comforting. It was chaos down there."

"Yep. Chaos. Scary and unknown, and sometimes nothing seems to make any sense. I figure jumping into the hole together is what brings the comfort. Staying the course together. Although so far, Rosie Jo, that's just a theory."

She understood what he was saying. He needed a partner to turn hypothesis to reality. He'd been ready for a while, waiting for her.

Though her mouth went dry, Rosemary spoke. "Let's test your theory." *Boom, boom, boom.* Her chest cavity felt like a kettledrum being played too hard. She swallowed hard around the pounding. "I'm willing to jump. With you."

Dean stared at her a long time. Then a grin broke like sunshine over his face. He threw back his head and whooped. It was loud, out of character and wonderful. She laughed as he whirled her around then kissed her before her feet hit the ground. After so many gray days, the future sparkled with color.

"Well, I'd like to meet my son-in-law." Maeve Jeffers's ever-determined voice broke into the festivities. "I assume this is he?"

Dean set Rosemary down and together they turned toward four women—Maeve, Rosemary's sisters, Lucy and Evelyn, and Vi—all of whom stared back with a decided mix of reactions. Rosemary's mother, the only attorney Rosemary knew who was scarier than Lucy, looked much the way she did when going after a deadbeat father in court; her sisters appeared faintly appalled, and Vi was amused.

"Hi, Mom," Rosemary greeted, hoping she could hang on to the good feelings despite an immediate flashback to the day two decades ago when her mother found her practicing the wedding march with a pillowcase bobby-pinned to her hair.

"Rosemary," Maeve had told her twelve-year-old romantic, not ungently, *"do you know that some of the world's great feminist writers have compared marriage to slavery?"*

Face-to-face with her daughter's second husband, Maeve extended her hand with a kind of militaristic grace. Like a marine sniper at high tea. "How do you do? I'm Maeve Jeffers, your new mother-in-law…apparently."

"Dean Kingsley." Dean accepted her hand graciously, glancing at Rosemary. "Luckiest man alive."

Despite the pleasure rush that engulfed her, Rosemary knew too well that Dean had just slapped a bull's eye on his own forehead. Her mother and sisters were always extrasuspicious of a man who appeared besotted and had the temerity to talk about it. At their cousin Madeline's wedding to a man who toasted his bride by tearfully quoting Elizabeth Barrett Browning, Lucy had leaned in to Rosemary and cracked, *"I'll be seeing him in court when he uses the child support to pay for his mistress's boob job."*

For the first time, Rosemary wasn't concerned about her relatives' opinions, not on her own behalf. They could think whatever the heck they wanted; she was happy, dang it! She did, however, feel a ferocious surge of protectiveness toward Dean.

Hugging her mother and sisters, Rosemary whispered, "Play nicely," and wondered how to draw Lucy aside to make sure her lawyer sister had kept mum about the prenup and

Rosemary's pregnancy. Lucy's thin body was as tense as piano wire, not an unusual state for her, but she appeared particularly stiff this evening.

Rosemary made bug eyes at Vi, hoping for a little inspiration about how to handle the moment, but Vi mouthed *Lotsa luck* and took an extralong swig of diet soda.

"You look lovely, Rosemary," Maeve admitted, scrutinizing her youngest daughter closely then turning her attention to Dean. "Do you mind if I pull you away from my daughter for a moment? I'd like to get to know you a little better before I head back to Portland."

"I'll come, too, Mom," Rosemary said immediately. "I haven't seen you in months."

"We're hoping you'll stay in Honeyford a few days," Dean added, including Evelyn and Lucy as well, which caused Vi to choke on her soda and Rosemary nearly to gag on her own spit.

"Unfortunately that won't be possible," Maeve declined. "I'm due in court on Monday and need to prepare. I'm going to put the screws to a multimillionaire who had the audacity to suggest his wife of twenty years should be happy with a lump-sum settlement that doesn't even reach seven figures." She smiled brightly at her new son-in-law. "Men can be so naive."

"Mom," Rosemary chastised at the blatant warning. *This* was what she'd had to overcome all her life in order to believe in romance.

Dean squeezed her waist and merely smiled. He'd asked about her family a couple of nights ago, and she hadn't held back. He'd laughed at some of the things she'd told him, winced at others and commiserated. He hadn't grown up in a Beaver Cleaver world, either. Though his parents' brief marriage had been happy, his father had apparently had a far more difficult second union. Dean had also divulged that the current *mayor* of Honeyford, Gwen Gibson, had been his father's mistress for many years.

"In the end, though, my father believed a committed marriage was the most important ingredient to happiness," Dean had surprised her by saying. *"I'm sure he wished he'd married Gwen. My father's problem was that he had no idea how to achieve the kind of marriage he believed in."*

For several moments after that conversation, Dean had seemed distracted, distant for the first time since she'd met him. Glancing at him now, she saw that he was plenty connected and assessing the situation with his new in-laws correctly.

With great politeness, he invited, "I'd love to have some time to know you better before you leave, Maeve. And, I'm sure you have a number of questions I'd be happy to answer." He squeezed Rosemary's waist again, a pointedly reassuring caress, and added, "Sweetheart, why don't you introduce your sisters around. I see Fletcher and Claire over by the fireplace."

"Fletcher?" Vi perked up. "Absolutely let's go see Fletcher. I've got my camera."

"Fletcher...Kinglsey?" Evelyn, the senior director of advertising at a firm that served the west coast from San Francisco to Anchorage, busily put two and two together. "Your brother-in-law is the Tuff Enuff jeans model?" she asked Rosemary.

Vi raised her can of soda. "Ain't life grand?"

"I'll tag along with Mom and Dean," Lucy announced, far more interested in interrogating a new victim than ogling a cowboy—or snagging him for an ad campaign, which Rosemary figured was Evelyn's angle.

Rosemary looked at Dean, undecided. Should she allow her mother and sister, two self-avowed man-distrusting divorce attorneys, to be alone with her new husband when there was no telling what kind of shape they'd leave him in?

She looked Dean square in the eye. He winked.

Team Kingsley vs. Team Jeffers, his expression said. *This one's a slam dunk.*

The silent communication made her feel more than ever like part of a couple, and her nervous heart settled.

All right, then, she winked back. *Good luck.*

All the while she stood beside Vi and Evelyn—and eventually Daphne and Ginger, who made their way over, too—as they pelted Fletcher with requests for photos and his agent's phone number, Rosemary knew she had found her needle in the haystack, the man who made her want to believe again.

Yesterday she had seen her obstetrician, making the two-hour round-trip trek to Bend for what she hoped would be the last time. Now that she and Dean were married she could see a doctor here in town. Maybe Dean would even come with her. There would be gossip, no doubt, when folks did the math, but if they knew that she and Dean loved each other...

Love. A grin spread across her face. After promising herself that never again would she have expectations of any man, here she was, expecting. Expecting like crazy! Expecting Dean's baby, expecting his friendship, expecting a lifetime together.

They had gone into this relationship entirely backward and had a lot of catching up to do. Thankfully they'd gotten a good head start: he was becoming a wonderful friend already.

Her thoughts a million miles away, she didn't notice her sister-in-law trying to catch her attention until Claire tugged her away from the group. "Fletcher says I shouldn't ask, but you look so happy I just have to. How are things? Are you and Dean enjoying marriage?" She put a hand to her mouth, adorably. "Oh, shoot, that sounds way too personal. Scratch that. Are you getting excited about the baby?"

Rosemary grinned. "I am. I really, really am."

"Do you know what you're having?"

Glancing around to be sure no one else could hear their conversation, Rosemary nodded. "I found out yesterday. I've been trying to think of a creative way to tell Dean."

Claire's eyes glowed with sweet remembering. "I loved that part—telling Arlo what we were going to have. I usually strung it out a good long while."

Dean had told Rosemary that Arlo was Claire's first husband. He'd died before their third child, Rosalind, had made her appearance. Rosemary could tell by Claire's expression and by the tone of her lovely Southern voice that her marriage to Arlo had been a good one. Now that the young woman (Rosemary guessed Claire to be several years younger than her own thirty-two) was in a second happy marriage, Rosemary wondered whether she and Fletcher would add a fourth child to their brood. She decided to ask and earned a sigh.

"Well, I have brought that up, and Fletcher has agreed to discuss it in ten years or so."

"Ten years," Rosemary laughed. "Oh, no. I was hoping for lots and lots of cousins for our little one."

Claire glanced lovingly at her husband, surrounded and looking none too thrilled about it, by Rosemary's sister and friends. "Well," Claire mused, "Fletcher is a new daddy still. He's in that deer-caught-in-the-headlights stage where he's afraid he'll make a mistake that will destroy the world as we know it. Poor baby dreamed last night that he dropped Will on his head. And Will's seven."

"No kidding." It was hard to believe they were talking about the six-foot-plus rodeo star. "Wasn't Fletcher a bull rider?"

"Yes. But I haven't met a bull yet that could bring a man to his knees quick as a baby can." Claire inched closer and lowered her voice even though the music and chatter would have made it hard for anyone to overhear their conversation. "Also you've got to remember that Fletcher and Dean's daddy left them fairly confused about what it takes to be a husband and father. It's hard to understand that man's motives, isn't it?"

Clueless, Rosemary didn't bother to mask her bemusement. "Sorry? I'm not sure what you mean by 'motives.' Motives for what?"

The change in Claire's expression was swift and more confusing than her comment. The cheerful openness from a moment before fled, replaced by a shuttered, uncertain look. "Oh, it was nothing. I don't know why I even brought it up." She looked at Fletcher...a little desperately, Rosemary thought. "I'd better rescue my husband. I wonder if your sister or one of your friends just used the word *model,* 'cause he's wincing like he's in a lot of pain."

Rosemary smiled, but watched curiously as Claire pulled her husband away. The girls began to animatedly discuss Fletcher's assets, but Rosemary's attention was halfhearted at best. When she found an appropriate moment to excuse herself, she took it.

Wandering the room in search of Dean proved to be futile. Every few steps, someone stopped her to chat, but no one knew where Dean had gone. Finally she came upon Irene Gould and Henry Berns, the owner of Honey Bea's Bakery.

Henry, a couple of inches shorter than Irene and obviously no more than a hundred and twenty pounds soaking wet, carried a full plate of food and was about to bite into a sauce-covered cabbage roll. Irene, who had known the little baker most of their lives, hovered over him. "Henry Berns, you're closer to eighty than eighteen. What are you thinking, eating like that?"

"Eighty? Speak for yourself. I may be no spring chicken, but I can still crow like a rooster." He winked at Rosemary, popped the cabbage roll in his mouth and scooped up kasha *varnishkas.*

Irene compressed her lips and turned to Rosemary.

"Congratulations, darling. So exciting. Marriage is a wonderful thing."

"How do you know?" Henry asked good-naturedly enough, scraping the plate with his fork.

Irene's eyes widened, shocked and, if Rosemary was correct, deeply hurt. "Why you old—" she began then clamped her lips shut. Her chest rose and fell heavily.

Rosemary's heart went out to her, but she had no idea how to help. *Major history there.* "Um, have either of you seen Dean recently?" she asked in the uncomfortable silence.

"He walked Gwen Gibson to her car," Irene informed stiffly, shooting a dagger-sharp glance at Henry. "*He's* a gentleman."

Ouch. "Thanks. I think I'll get a breath of fresh air myself."

The little baker looked up. "What do you mean, 'He's a gentleman'? Are you saying I'm not a gentleman?"

Yikes. With a wave, Rosemary left the two to whatever they had to work out and threaded through the crowd, escaping finally to the brisk spring night.

Embedded in the clear sky, stars winked more brightly than the twinkle lights in the community hall. Stretching her arms, Rosemary breathed deeply, thinking about the scene that had just transpired. Relationships were so complex. Did anyone find her way through the maze unscathed?

A powerful need to see her husband, to feel the comfort of his solid arms and his eminently reassuring calmness, arose in Rosemary. She squinted in the darkness. Cars had been parked along the curbless street, beside old hitching posts that remained from horse-and-buggy days. A black iron streetlamp flickered, shedding just enough light to see by, but there was no sign of Dean.

Realizing she should have grabbed a coat, Rosemary hugged her arms and made her way around the corner to the small parking lot behind the community center. It was nice of Dean to walk Gwen Gibson to her car. Rosemary had met the mayor twice—once shortly after she'd been hired to run the library, and once when Ms. Gibson had checked out a book on civic government. Nice lady. Widowed. Probably around sixty, she came across as very poised, with a comfortable elegance and a truckload of natural charm. She'd been in a long, somewhat tumultuous relationship with Dean's father, and though she'd married someone else and had a college-age son from that relationship, she and Victor Kingsley had become, at the very least, good friends again at the end of his life. Dean seemed to like and respect the woman, which was enough to make Rosemary more than happy to get to know Gwen better.

Before she'd completely rounded the brick building, Rosemary heard a female voice.

"It's incredible the way everything's worked out, isn't it? First for Fletcher and now for you."

The masculine response seemed to rumble through her own chest. "I couldn't have asked for it to turn out better."

Rosemary smiled. *Found you.* She felt her body relax even as anticipation fizzed along her nerves. *I'm like a teenager,* she thought with sappy surrender, *happy just to be getting closer to my guy.* She picked up her pace, but before she reached the parking lot, Gwen spoke again. This time, the words made Rosemary stumble on the gravel.

"I was so afraid your father's will was going to cause a disaster. I don't have to tell you how much I loved Victor, but requiring you to marry to gain an inheritance was incredibly risky. I knew you'd be more tolerant of the situation than Fletcher, but honestly, I thought the will might deter you both from ever marrying."

Rosemary's brain began to spin inside her skull. She reached reflexively for the brick wall, but her hand only scraped its rough surface. For several moments she couldn't see, couldn't hear, couldn't think. Then the words just spoken collided with the puzzling comment Claire had made, and her mind filled so horribly with dark thoughts she almost screamed.

She had the presence of mind to do one thing—back away. Stumbling a little, feeling her way along the wall as her legs turned to jelly, she reached the front of the community center. Go back inside? Not possible. Whirling left, adrenaline kicking in, propelling her like a hunted deer, she headed for the cover of the building on the other side of the driveway. *Good choice, Rosemary. Keep moving, keep moving.* Grateful for the Western-style building's deep porch, she headed for its farthest reaches, leaned against the rough wooden facade and hyperventilated.

God in heaven, she couldn't have made a mistake of such magnificent proportions. She couldn't be so wrong, so blind about a man, about their relationship.... Could she? Not this time, not...

With a baby on the way.

Her thoughts progressed to near hysteria.

Dean had married her because of a will. Gwen knew. Claire knew! And how many others?

Rosemary buried her head in her hands. "No, no, no." Things like this didn't happen to people in the real world; they happened on soap operas and *Jerry Springer* episodes and in nightmares.

Sobs built inside her, but she refused to let them gain power. She needed every wit she possessed. Lifting her head, she felt her heart buck as Dean walked around the community center, his shadowed form as tall and straight as ever.

Liar. Fake. Criminal.

If what she'd heard held even a kernel of truth then there were no words bad enough for what he'd done, for the way he'd misled and encouraged her to trust in him. For the way he'd made her love again.

I have to talk to Lucy. I have to dissolve this marriage!

A car rolled out of the parking lot and down the block. Gwen Gibson, the mayor of their fair town. *"I don't have to tell you how much I loved your father."* The Kingsleys wove a large and tangled web.

The town that had seemed like such a haven mere minutes ago now felt about as wholesome as Wisteria Lane.

"I've got to get out of here." Rosemary struggled for breath as Dean disappeared inside the community center. *Run. Run as fast and as far as you can.*

Two years ago Rosemary was supposed to have worked on the evening of her tenth wedding anniversary, which had been her birthday, too, because Neil, bless him, had insisted, "I want to get married on the day God made the perfect woman for me."

When her boss had let her go home early, she'd made reservations at their favorite restaurant and rushed home to surprise him. He'd looked surprised, all right. Naked, having sex on their couch with his paralegal, and surprised.

Rosemary had been too stunned to say a word. She'd simply run out the door while Neil yelled after her, "I didn't use our bed, Rosemary!"

That was true: he hadn't used their bed—that time. During their divorce, however, there had been a steady stream of informants, more than willing to assure her that divorce was the right decision, that her husband had been cheating on her for years.

Slowly Rosemary walked to the edge of the porch, hot now despite the chill night air. She had loved Neil once, would never have suspected him capable of such treachery, yet even during their marriage she had known there was something missing, an elusive, soul-deep sense of…rightness…of completion, a click for which she had reached and reached before finally telling herself it would come with age.

Then she met Dean. What had scared—and thrilled—her most that first night was that she had felt the click the first time his eyes had crinkled at her.

Tears gathered, then began to squirt like projectiles.

Blast. She pressed a hand over her mouth and prayed for calm, for composure, for a shot of Novocain straight to the heart. What lesson, damn it, was she supposed to be learning?

Don't run.

As if the voice were outside her, loud and clear, she heard the message: *Stop running. Stand and face up to your life. Face your dreams, even the ones that are broken, and for pity's sake, face the sonofabitch who's breaking them.*

Stock-still, but panting as if she'd broken the tape in a marathon, Rosemary waited for her mind to catch up with that voice.

She'd fallen in love. Again. More wildly than before. And unfortunately, being duped didn't change that fact.

Now she was going to have a daughter to raise. That was the news she'd planned to give Dean tonight. They were having a baby girl. And no matter what her mama told her, that baby girl that would someday be a young woman who yearned to love and be loved. What could Rosemary teach her? What kind of role model would she be?

Just don't run.

Maybe she couldn't keep her daughter's heart safe or pain-free. Of course she couldn't. If Maeve and all her preaching against the myth of the romantic fairy tale hadn't worked, what would?

Not a damn thing, probably.

Like Rosemary, her daughter would choose her own path to tread. God willing, she'd be lucky. As for Rosemary…

"I'm done."

There was only one thing left to do, as far as she could tell. Wiping her eyes, she sniffed hard. Time to be a big girl, broken or not.

Rosemary headed resolutely toward the building where her wedding reception was still going strong despite the fact the marriage had tanked. Her family and friends were in there. They'd driven three hours to celebrate with her; she wasn't going to abandon them. No. She was going to go back in there and finish this reception. In style.

Allowing a moment's grief for the loss of the beautiful future she had planned, Rosemary sucked it up and kept walking. She couldn't stay in Honeyford after this. The details of where she would move and when could be settled in the light of day. Right now, she had a surprise for the man who had turned her dream to dust. It was time to toast the groom…or turn the groom to toast.

Chapter Fourteen

Something was wrong. Damn wrong.

For the past hour, Dean had watched his bride work the room—her smile wide and ready, her gaze sharp, her laughter bold. But to him, she looked like a piece of crystal—solid and beautiful, yet teetering on the edge of a table over a hardwood floor, about to shatter at any minute. Worse, she wouldn't let him get anywhere near her.

Five minutes ago he'd spotted her dancing with his nephew Will. As he began to make his way through the crowd, which hadn't thinned a hair since the start of the evening, Rosemary glanced up, ignored his smile and twirled Will over to her friend Vi. Then she whispered something in the redhead's ear and took off without another glance in Dean's direction.

Enough was definitely enough, so he'd pressed after her, but Len had stopped him, having a *manic* (man in panic) attack, because Daphne had just revealed that she planned to be celibate until she met her future husband, no matter how long it took. "She thinks a man's going to go for that? Partner, that's like saddling a racehorse then putting it in the barn."

It had taken a few minutes to calm Len down. Now Dean was looking for Rosemary again.

A loud, amplified whistle rent the air. "Ladies and gentleman, may I have your attention, please? Up here."

Dean turned toward the far end of the hall, where the band played on a raised stage. Eugene Brock, former sheriff and current lead guitarist of Crystallized Honey, was speaking into the mike. Rosemary stood next to him, looking nervous, but brave.

"Folks, we're here to celebrate another couple God put together right here in Honeyford. Now it happens that the very last time we were here in this room 'cause of a wedding, Dean's brother, Fletcher, had just tied the knot. Seems like the Kingsleys are having more than their fair share of luck this year."

Laughter and ribbing erupted from the crowd. "Yeah!" Reginald Jacobson, who owned a small sheep ranch outside of town, hollered, "Two pretty women move to town, and the Kingsleys get 'em both. What's up with that? The next one's mine!"

"Well, soon as you take care of that comb-over, Reg, I believe you'll have better luck." More hooting followed Eugene's comment. He patted the air to calm everyone down. "We've got to give our attention to the guest of honor here. The brand-spankin'-new Mrs. Kingsley would like to make a toast." Detaching the microphone from its stand, he handed it to Rosemary. "Mrs. Kingsley, the floor is yours."

Dean tensed as his wife accepted the mike with a nod and a deep breath. Shouldn't he be up there with her? One of Claire's more elaborate cakes had been carried out and placed on the end of the buffet table. He'd assumed they would make their toasts while cutting the tiered creation. Perhaps Rosemary wanted to surprise him, and that's what her avoidance had been about. He began to move toward the stage, this time propelled by shoulder slaps.

As he reached the steps leading to where his wife stood, their gazes locked. Instead of the melting sugar look he expected...wanted...to see, Rosemary's brow puckered. Her lids lowered, narrowing her expression to a cloud-covered puzzle. He stopped walking, remained at the foot of the steps and knew instantly she wanted it that way.

Instead of inviting her husband onto the stage, Rosemary raised the microphone, turned toward the crowd and gave them a smile they may have believed was genuine, but which he realized went no further than the stretch of her lips.

"Thank you." She acknowledged the former sheriff then expelled a breath that reverberated in the mike. "Thank you all for coming." Taking a moment, she centered herself, looking poised and self-possessed as the toast began. "It's no secret that I arrived in Honeyford a single woman. Yet now here I am, very unexpectedly married." Happy applause punctuated the comment. She nodded to recognize it. "Some might say I let Dean sweep me off my feet—" increased cheerful hollers "—or that we rushed things. And maybe that's true."

Her eyes skittered toward his again. Dean felt his heart drop heavily toward his gut. What the hell... Her glance was brief. Brittle.

He considered this one of the most important nights in his life. Earlier today he had contacted his father's lawyer, instructing him to sell the building on Main Street to the city of Honeyford for the bargain-basement price of one dollar. The only stipulation was that he be allowed to lease the space occupied by the pharmacy for the next ten years and that Clinica Adelina be allowed to lease the two neighboring storefronts at current market value for the same period of time. He'd told Gwen as much this evening when he'd walked her to her car.

She was the executor of the will and believed, as he did, that the city would go for the terms. Because he had married in time to meet the will's demands, he held the cards. What they didn't have to know was that he would relinquish the building no matter what. He couldn't conduct this marriage under the shadow of his father's will.

All his life Dean had tried to do the right thing. Now the "right thing" was whatever it took to make his relationship with Rosemary work.

So that glance of hers, sharp as glass, raised an alarm in his head. He met her eyes with a question in his own.

"The thing is," she said, again addressing the room, managing to look poised yet vulnerable, "all my life I wanted to marry a man I knew would never let me down. A man I could trust, because his word would be as good as gold, and his love…" for a breath of space, her voice hovered before she completed the thought "…his love would be immovable. I wanted to look into his eyes and know that the man I loved when I was thirty would be standing beside me fifty years later. And nothing would have changed except the lines on our faces." She looked at the crowd of neighbors, friends and family, her smile inviting their comradeship and offering her own. "When you get down to it, that's what most of us are looking for, isn't it? To know that the person we go to sleep beside each night will be in our corner the next day?"

Dean heard a feminine sniffle. In his mind, a bull's eye began to take shape on his back.

His own brother, formerly the devil incarnate, had pointed out that Dean had been lying by omission for the duration of his relationship with Rosemary. Now he stared at his wife, at the hazel eyes that looked like a lake on fire, and though he had no idea what had transpired between their dance and this moment, he knew she delivered no ordinary toast.

Rosemary held the microphone with both hands. "Some

people—people in my own family, even—" she grinned to minimize any implied judgment "—say true love is a fairy tale. That to keep from falling down, a strong woman has to stand up alone. Well, to tell you the truth, after surviving a broken heart once, I was all set to agree with them. I even told my friends I wasn't going to date again. *Ever*." More laughter from their guests. Rosemary nodded. "I know, I know. You speak, the universe laughs. And, of course, then I met Dean." As the chuckles died down, she lowered her voice, sounding almost wistful. "I never expected to meet someone so caring. So willing to put other people first. So deeply, deeply moral. I don't mind telling you that at first I thought he was too good to be true. And I decided to keep my distance. But that Dean, he's a persistent—" she paused, slightly but significantly "—devil. When I married him, I knew that with a man like him, I could put my fears to rest." Her eyes cut to her husband, who felt her gaze like the point of a saber aimed at his heart. "Because Dean Kingsley—the honest, up-front man you all know, the Prince Charming I had started to believe didn't exist—that man would never, ever, *willingly* let me fall."

There was more sniffling. Rosemary raised her glass of punch, and while their guests drank, she and Dean looked at each other with one thing crystal clear between them: the honeymoon was over. In spades.

Rosemary pressed her shoulder against the Prius's passenger-side door, gazing out the window at the clear, sharp night. They'd left the party five minutes ago; it was almost 11:00 p.m.

In the driver's seat—literally, but most definitely not figuratively—Dean had been mostly silent. He hadn't said much at all, in fact, since her toast, and she wasn't sure whether she was glad or angrier than ever.

Now as they neared her cottage, he asked, "Do you want to talk now or wait until we get home?"

If she were a porcupine, he'd be covered in quills right now. When she'd discovered the extent of Neil's cheating, Rosemary had left her house and hadn't returned. She'd let Neil live there until they'd sold the lovely Lake Oswego three-bedroom in the divorce settlement. Not this time. The cottage belonged to her, and she was no pushover. Not anymore.

"My home is on 4th Street," she said quietly but firmly. "Yours is above the pharmacy." They would have to talk, yes, but she wanted the ground rules established: the marriage, as they had so briefly known it, was over.

Still a couple of blocks from the house, Dean pulled over and cut the engine. He turned toward her. "Who told you?"

"Who told me what, Dean? What is there to tell? Honeyford's favorite son is an open book, right?"

"Rosie—"

She held her hand up between them. "Refrain from using nicknames or endearments, please. These days they tend to make me gag."

Dean kept a hand on the steering wheel. His knuckles tightened around it, whitening. He shook his head. "I'm an ass. Whether you believe it or not, Rosie—" She glared at him. "Rosemary—I was going to tell you about my father's will tonight."

"You were going to tell me *tonight*. After our wedding reception." She blinked, affecting a broad smile. "Gosh, that makes all the difference. Thanks. Oh, wait." She began counting off points on her fingers. "Four months after we slept together, two months after you found out I was pregnant and almost three weeks after we got married, you were just going to tell me that according to your father's will you *had* to get married. Ooh, you know what? I'm not that grateful, after all." She shrugged broadly. "Sorry." Dropping the sarcasm, she went for the jugular. "What is the matter with you? What kind of person does something like this? Who gets married because of a will? And *deceives* people about it?" The interior of the small car filled with her wrath. She had plenty more to say, but then remembered something. "Oh, my god. Amanda found out about the will, didn't she? That's why she broke up with you."

"Amanda did not break up with me." Twisting as fully as he could toward Rosemary, Dean said, carefully and clearly, "I broke up with her, because when I saw you again I knew I couldn't marry anyone else. Amanda was aware of the will from the start. She wasn't in love with me."

Rage, hot and furious, exploded within her, and Rosemary kept her arms rigidly by her side so she wouldn't attack him. Never in her life, not even with Neil, had she felt so outraged, so dangerously furious.

"I don't know Amanda, I didn't know your father, and I obviously *don't know you,* but it's clear that not one of you understands or cares that marriage is something sacred, not a game. You don't play with it, and you don't mess with other people's lives."

Dean's face knotted with regret and contrition. He looked so aggrieved, in fact, that she might have comforted him if she hadn't wanted, at that moment, to turn his male parts into pudding.

"Rosie—" he began. Once more channeling one of the witches in *Macbeth,* she raised a brow. "Rosemary," he corrected, "only a handful of people know about my father's will. I'm not sure who told you—"

"Nobody told me," she said, omitting what she now recognized as a slip on Claire's part, earlier. She didn't want to involve anyone else in this mess. "I was coming to look for you and overheard Gwen Gibson say how beautifully everything had worked out for you and Fletcher. Imagine my surprise when I heard the mayor congratulate my husband on his *forced* marriage."

Dean closed his eyes briefly, swearing beneath his breath. "I'm sorry. That isn't what I intended—" He stopped as a new realization dawned. "Wait. If you overheard Gwen and me then you—" He shook his head. "You didn't stay for the whole conversation, did you?"

"No. Although, golly, that would have been fun. What'd you two talk about next? Insurance scams? Pyramid schemes?"

Dean did not answer. He merely started the car again, and Rosemary was glad. Sarcasm was not her usual modus operandi. She felt as if an alien force had taken over her tongue, and she was already sick of it, sick of the hatred she felt. She wanted to be done.

Exhaustion, as swift and global as her fury, drained her. When Dean passed her cottage without stopping, it took her a moment to react.

"What are you doing? Go back, please. I want to go home."

Dean didn't look at her. "We're going to see Gwen." He set his jaw as if steeling himself to press forward no matter what.

"I don't want to see anyone, and it's eleven p.m. I doubt Gwen will be happy to see us."

Dean turned right on Oak Street then made a left on Second, heading for an area of lovely old Victorians. "You heard a fraction of our conversation," he said. "You're not going to believe anything I tell you right now, and I don't blame you. So you're going to hear the rest of it from Gwen." He stared forward, through the windshield again, his face illuminated by the occasional streetlamp. "From the second I saw you, I felt differently about you than I've felt about any other woman in my life. I didn't tell you the truth right away, because—" Now he glanced her way. "How the hell do you tell someone your father's will requires you to marry? I was afraid I'd lose you before we ever got started."

Through the darkness, Rosemary saw the turbulence in his usually pacific blue eyes. Emotion roughened his voice like sandpaper. "I didn't want to lose you, Rosie. So I tried to control everything, and you're right—I screwed up. But you're mistaken about one thing. Kingsley men do value marriage. Fletcher and I valued it to the point that we were too scared to make a move toward it. Our father valued it so much, he tried to force us into it. The problem isn't that we don't want love—it's that we haven't got the faintest idea how to make it work."

They pulled up in front of a grand home with only one small light glowing from an upstairs room. Dean cut the engine and opened his door.

"It really is too late to disturb someone," Rosemary protested mildly, trying vainly to digest everything that had happened tonight and all Dean had just told her.

He came around to her side, opened the door and bent down to look at her. "It *is* too late to disturb someone. And maybe what Gwen is going to tell you won't matter in the end. But I'm not giving you—or our family—up without a fight, Rosemary Kingsley. The only ammunition I've got left is the truth."

He stepped back, letting Rosemary decide what it was going to be: end things here or listen to what Gwen Gibson had to say.

Life seemed so ridiculously complex, so unbearably painful that Rosemary wanted to run from all of it. Even as she tried to steel herself against Dean, her heart thumped against her chest as if it were trying to move closer to him. She wanted to listen, wanted him to reassure and convince her that this issue of the will and a forced marriage was all some big misunderstanding.

Magical thinking.

She tried to remember that she had just left three friends, two sisters and a mother, all of whom were single and in a lot less pain than she was in right now.

Dean waited at the curb, his expression as intent as she had ever seen it. Anxious finger-combing had mussed his usually neat hair.

Not two hours ago, you were my knight in shining armor, and I was lucky in love, Rosemary thought with a sadness that penetrated her bones.

When she got out of the car, it was not with hope, precisely, but rather with the weary conviction that if nothing else, perhaps Gwen Gibson would weave the loose threads of this insane tapestry together.

As she stepped onto the curb, Rosemary looked into Dean's troubled eyes.

The only ammunition I've got is the truth, he'd said.

Truth was good. Maybe truth was all she needed. Because she certainly sensed she was finished with fairy tales, forevermore.

Lucy Jeffers sat on the floor of her sister's living room, picking food from a plate on the coffee table, which currently was set like a Thanksgiving buffet.

"Thanks for coming over and bringing…a snack." Rosemary pushed a halfhearted smile her sister's way. Because Lucy never ate junk food, she had arrived at Rosemary's door with a whole roasted chicken from the market, a quart of wild-rice pilaf, salad, rolls, a Dutch apple pie, a pesto-crusted cheese ball and water crackers.

Eschewing the real food, Rosemary had curled into a corner of the couch with an open bag of cheese puffs—the natural kind, because she refused to feed the baby anything fluorescent, but still something that resembled food therapy. She was depressed, miserable, wretched; roasted chicken and a green vegetable were not going to cut it.

"I still can't believe you stayed in town after Mom and Evelyn left," Rosemary said, watching her sister carefully remove all visible fat from a bite of poultry. "How was the Honeyford Inn?"

"Good. They put me in the honeymoon suite, though." She snorted. "What a crock." Jamming a fork into the meat with unnecessary aggression, Lucy put the chicken in her mouth and chewed as if the bird still needed to be killed.

"Um, why did you stay exactly?"

Lucy looked up. "My sister having a nervous breakdown onstage at her wedding reception isn't a good enough reason?"

"I wasn't having a nervous breakdown," Rosemary protested, hugging her cheese puffs. Apparently the veiled irony in her little toast hadn't been so veiled, after all. Daphne had phoned her three times on the trip back to Portland and once since. Vi had videotaped most of the toast with her cell phone and threatened to post it on YouTube unless Rosemary called to tell her exactly what was going on. "You, Mom and Evelyn should be proud of me," Rosemary protested in a wobbly voice that sounded dangerously like whining. "I was refusing to be a patsy."

"We are proud. It was just hard to figure out what was going on last night. 'Oh, wow, my sister must have found out her husband had to marry her to inherit a building' is not the first thing that crosses your mind before the wedding cake is cut, you know?" Picking walnuts out of the wild-rice pilaf, Lucy raised a skinny brow, dark as soot against her pale skin. "Unbe*effing*lievable that he thought he'd get away with it. *Putz.*"

Squirming painfully on the sofa she had purchased originally for its uncommon comfort, Rosemary reminded Lucy dejectedly, "Except that he wasn't trying to 'get away with it.' Remember? I told you, Gwen confirmed that he's selling his building to the city. He just wanted to keep the will quiet as long as possible, because he knew there was no way to explain it to me so that it would make any kind of sense." *Gee, put that way—*

"Don't romanticize him, Rosemary," Lucy snapped, and Rosemary jumped guiltily.

"I'm not romanticizing him. He still lied to me…by omission…for months, and…that's a deal breaker."

"Damn straight. Because if a man lies once, he'll do it again. Men are such shmucks." Abandoning the wild rice, Lucy plunged her fork into the Dutch apple pie.

Rosemary stared. "Luce, is there something *you* need to talk about? I mean, other than my being duped into a marriage of convenience, did something else happen to make you take this…vacation?"

Filling her mouth with apples and streusel topping, Lucy affected an amazed expression. "What? No. I am here for you."

"Luce—"

"I said, no! Look, it's no big deal." She shoveled in more pie, expanding her normally gaunt cheeks. "One of the partners at my firm got engaged, and his fiancée—" shifting from apple pie, she aimed her fork-weapon at the cheese ball "—joined the firm. Like being around each other 24/7 is going to contribute to marital bliss. Whatever. Anyway, no time like the present to claim some unused vacation time now that Lindsay the Perfect is there to pick up the slack. Not that there was any slack, because, of course, I have busted my butt for that ma—that firm practically my entire adult working life. But that's okay, because now there's plenty of lawyers on board to cover any emergency, so I can have a—" she looked as if she was going to cry or spit "—vacation."

Stunned, Rosemary poked as gently as she could at her sister's huge, gaping, utterly unexpected wound. "Was Dustin Phillips the lawyer who got engaged?"

Lucy had worked for Dustin's father's firm since her college internship. Dustin was very into civic action, and Lucy had hammered nails alongside him for Habitat for Humanity. Five years ago, Rosemary noted that her sister hadn't been able to take her eyes off Dustin at the annual Phillips, Phillips, Arnold & Locke company softball game. She'd hovered around him, fetched bats and lemonade, laughed too loudly, nodded too hard. Rosemary had wondered then if her sister was finally smitten, but Evelyn had insisted Lucy was merely trying to score points with the boss.

Now tears filled Lucy's eyes, an occurrence about as frequent as a Sasquatch sighting. She tried heroically to sniff them back.

"Aw, gee, Luce." Rosemary made to rise, but her sister shook her head, using the side of her fork to massacre the cheese ball.

"Don't romanticize it, Rosemary."

Right.

Sinking back into the corner of her couch, Rosemary tugged the collar of her sweatshirt up over her chin and sighed. Lord knew that in the Jeffers family romanticizing anything—men, women, snow geese that were faithful for life—was a sin punishable by a lifetime of regrets. Hadn't Rosemary proved that point? Twice?

Releasing the sweatshirt, she plunged her hand into the cheese puffs, stuffing a handful of their all-natural selves into her mouth.

After descending on Gwen, she and Dean had returned to the cottage. Midnight had come and gone with Dean explaining how conflicted he had been about relinquishing the building, how responsible he felt for the success of Clinica

Adelina and how that had informed his original decision to comply with his father's nutty will.

"I'd never been in love. Not really." He had looked sad and gorgeous, like Hubbell Gardner telling Katie Morosky he couldn't be what she needed in *The Way We Were*. "I honestly thought there was something broken inside me. So I resigned myself to a marriage that was sensible and figured everyone would be happy, myself included...or happy enough."

Too agitated to sit despite the late hour, Dean had logged multiple laps across the living-room floor while Rosemary huddled on the sofa in her reception dress, her brain hurting from confusion, her hands ice-cold though the gas fireplace hissed and blazed. "Then I went to Tavern on the Highway and saw you, licking salt off the pretzels and trying to be cheerful for your friends.... You were the most beautiful thing I'd ever seen."

He had stopped dead center of the couch, gazing at her with sorrow and longing, making her wish they were upstairs, spooned with one of his big, warm hands on her breast and the other on her belly, the way they had been for a small collection of the most delicious nights of her life.

"I wish I knew how to love you better." His voice cracked. "The way you deserve to be loved. I'm not even sure what that means, that's the damn truth of it."

It was the most vulnerable statement she'd heard a man utter. Though her body felt stiff and as fragile, she had wanted to hurl herself off the couch and into his arms. To kiss and reassure him that she had enough trust and courage for the both of them.

He said he loves you, the romantic in her encouraged. *You'll be all better now. You'll be fine.* They would make love every night, spend weekends at the coast, go on a hundred second honeymoons—

Stop. No one present said, "I love you." The practical,

Jeffers side of her gave the romantic one upside the head, knocking her off her fluffy cloud. *That's beside the point, anyway, isn't it? Do you want the pain that comes with the kind of love you're mooning about? You think your heart's going to keep beating when it's that swollen and sore? When Dean lets you down or lies or decides he doesn't l-o-v-e you anymore? Will you be glad then that you tried again? Right, didn't think so.*

Instead of diving for Dean's chest, Rosemary had stared at her husband of three weeks, her heart shuddering like an engine struggling to keep working just before it ran out of gas. Her throat had ached and suddenly she'd wished she had spent her thirty-second birthday at a Buddhist monastery or a verbal-fast retreat on Whidbey Island or just about anywhere but Tavern on the Highway.

Instead of reliving last night's final moments with Dean, Rosemary now demanded of her sister, "Tell me about Frank." *Frank.* They never referred to the man who had sired them as Father. Or Dad, Daddy, Pop or any other name that might identify him as family. "Tell me about the day he left."

Lucy coughed, spitting a little cheese onto the table. She swore beneath her breath. "God, Rosemary, what is it with you? Ever since we were kids, you've wanted to hear about it like it's a freaking bedtime story or something."

"I want to remember."

"What for? It's not one of your fairy tales."

"I know that." Not that there was anything wrong with the fairy tales that, yes, okay, had given her hope and comfort during the dark childhood fears. Fairy tales were kind… ultimately. The bad stuff happened mostly before the declaration of true love. Once the hero and heroine found each other, you knew nothing would tear them asunder. Ever. Sure, Cinderella had to return to the cellar and wait for the townies to try on her shoe, but that was a small price to pay for lifelong devotion, a castle full of adorable singing mice and, eventually, babies.

On the other hand, Lucy had a point. Rosemary did like to hear the story—in excruciating, full-color detail—of the day her father had left their family for good. For decades now, she had examined the fine points like a CSI picking over evidence, sure she'd find something that could have prevented the crime.

Had she been in charge of the situation, she might have found a word, a touch, a promise to alter the outcome. She'd clung to that idea, using it to convince herself that she could dodge the land mines of pain that had detonated in the wake of her parents' divorce.

I romanticize everything, because reality scares the crap out of me.

Clutching the bag of cheese puffs like a teddy bear, she stared, wide-eyed, at her sister. "Luce, do you think you, Evelyn and I might be in good relationships today if we'd grown up in a healthy family? Or do you think everyone gets driven through the wringer when they love someone? I mean, I used to think people who were compatible and madly in love had easier relationships. But lately I wonder if it's this hard for everyone, and some people just have a higher pain tolerance."

With a look that begged the universe to stop the torture, Lucy, previously her nutritionist's star client, ripped a white roll in half, shoved the entire piece into her mouth and chased it with pie. "Thith ith the motht deprething aftuhnoon evuh," she mumbled through the mouthful.

Rosemary sighed. With Dean standing before her, openly confused and vulnerable—not at all the absolutely certain, fear-slaying, unequivocal man she'd always imagined—she had panicked.

Wait. Rewind that. She'd been panicking all her life, and with Dean in front of her, as perplexed by relationships as she was, she hadn't known what to do with her fear. Neil had always told her not to worry. About anything. Prince Charming was supposed to kill the nasty dragons, right?

That is so yesterday, the Jeffers voice taunted. *Remember—*

"I know, I know. Don't romanticize."

She had believed the right man would provide a lifetime guarantee. But that kind of thinking was as magical as believing she could protect herself from pain by remaining alone.

She shook her head. Real life was about as clean as an oil spill. Last night, when faced with the possibility of accepting Dean and their marriage as the works in progress they were, she had cowered on the sofa and whispered, "I can't. I'm sorry. I just…can't."

Dean had stayed at his apartment above the pharmacy last night, and Rosemary, confused and conflicted, had slept not a wink.

Okay, big girl, it's time to face facts: if you want a guarantee, go shopping. Relationships do not come with the Good Housekeeping Seal. More's the pity, but there ya go.

Wow. That wasn't the Jeffers or the romantic voice. It was just…her.

Perhaps a person could hedge her bets by falling for someone who was as willing as she to keep the fires burning during the tough times or when love temporarily went MIA. Someone who believed in relationships and fidelity and trust. And by learning to forgive when one—or both—of them messed up.

Someone like Dean.

"I've got to go," she breathed.

"Wha?" Lucy lifted her head from the container of salad. "Where?" Understanding dawned. "No! Don't you dare. I…I…forbid it!"

Rosemary cocked her head. "Seriously?"

Lucy's customary certainty faltered. "Yes. I'm your sister and…your lawyer."

Smiling gratefully, Rosemary tucked the bag of cheese puffs between the chicken and the apple pie then rose, slipped her feet into purple flip-flops and headed for the door.

"Oh, God. Oh, God." Lucy, who made feral cats look relaxed by comparison, half rose, sat back down and rose again. "Change your clothes, at least," she called after her baby sister. "And brush your hair!"

"No time! But thanks."

Grabbing a set of keys off a hook and her Oregon Ducks cap from the coat tree near the door, Rosemary smashed the hat onto her head, unfortunately making her curls stick out like clown hair, and raced into the spring afternoon with Lucy's conflicted "Good luck" following her out the door.

Chapter Fifteen

Because the pharmacy was closed on Sundays, Rosemary took the alley staircase to Dean's apartment, hoping he was there. If not, her plan was to let herself in with the key he'd given her and wait. Regarding what she would say… Uh, yeah, not a clue.

Her heart, which had done more emotional aerobics these past few months than ever before in its life, thumped with nerves and excitement. She was nearly five months along in her pregnancy and had thrown on leggings with an oversize Oregon Shakespeare Festival T-shirt that masked her growing tummy, but did nothing for her fashion sense. Oh, well. If Dean wasn't there, then she'd take the time to freshen up a bit, maybe scrunch some gel, if he had any, into her curls while she waited.

Reaching the landing, glad there was no one else in the alley this afternoon, Rosemary raised her hand to knock on the glass-paned door. Noticing a movement inside, she hesitated, pressing her nose closer to the glass. Her busy heart skidded to a momentary halt.

Dean was inside the apartment, tall and handsome and tempting as always. But he wasn't alone.

"What?" Rosemary breathed, blinking as if she could make the scene inside disappear.

Seated on the leather couch that faced the alley windows, Dean gazed at an exotically beautiful woman as she leaned toward him, speaking animatedly.

Instantly, Rosemary reverted to the little girl who'd wondered endlessly why her father hadn't stayed. And to the wife who felt betrayed and foolish when her "perfect" life had turned out to be nothing more than an empty shell.

The urge to bolt came on strong. In the past twenty-four hours, she had gathered enough circumstantial evidence against Dean to write him off for good. If Lucy were here with her fork, she'd stab first and ask questions later. But the evidence was only circumstantial.

Fortunately for Dean, she was not one of her sisters. Or her mother. Or her friends. She was, finally, just Rosemary, and she knew exactly what she needed to do.

Her entire girlhood had been steeped in the quiet and desperate fear that she might end up alone. Her adulthood until two years ago—an exhausting exercise in trying to keep that from happening. More recently she'd attempted to tame the anxiety by convincing herself she embraced being alone.

Now she dived straight into the heart of the terror and discovered something amazing: the longer she stood inside it without flinching, the more it dissolved, like clouds. Behind the fear was the far more substantial soul she had never learned to trust.

Rosemary raised the hand holding the apartment key. Her other hand drifted to her abdomen, eyes narrowing speculatively as she patted the baby. "I can't fix the past, but I can do things differently now. Watch this, kiddo. Mama's going to show you how it's done."

Slipping the key into the lock, she moved swiftly, claiming the element of surprise as she burst into Dean's living room.

The gorgeous Latina woman with the sexy, straight black hair jumped, as did Dean, although when he saw who the intruder was, his surprise turned to, at first, concern and then bemusement. And finally, hope.

He stood, his attention all on Rosemary. The last thing he'd said to her the night before was, *"I'll be waiting. For as long as it takes you to forgive me, I'll wait."*

This afternoon all he managed was a surprised and questioning, "Rosie?"

She almost felt sorry for him. If he expected a quick and easy reunion this afternoon, he was in for a bit of a shock. *I've got a much better plan than that.*

Stomping forward, she halted only when her knees hit the coffee table then stabbed her index finger at Dean's admirable chest.

"Don't you 'Rosemary' me, bub. I come over here to bring you home, and what do I find?"

The woman, who really was lovely, jumped to her feet. "Oh, no! No, this is not what you're thinking—"

"Save it, sister." Adopting a growl that had never before emerged from her mouth, Rosemary realized that the poor woman was ready to whip out her iPhone and key in 9-1-1. *Sorry,* she tried to communicate telepathically. *But I have to make a point here.*

Gesturing toward her husband, she said, "That is *my* man. *Mine.* And I don't share."

"Oh, but, really, I'm not—"

Rosemary gave her a talk-to-the-hand. "Please," she said. "Believe me, I understand *why* you want him." Dean deserved some grandstanding after all he'd been through the past couple of days, and, by golly, he was going to get it. "He's gentle, he's kind, he's incredibly patient. Except for a little trust issue regarding his father's will and my ability to love him in spite of it—and I do love him in spite of it—the man is near perfect."

She turned to Dean, and their gazes locked. "Perfect enough for me, anyway. It took a while for me to figure out that I can't put my faith in anyone else until I've put it in myself, but I think I get that now. And just for the record, I like that you haven't fallen in love easily in your life." She smiled, her heart in her words and in her eyes. "Because I know this one's for real."

She paused, wanting to soak in Dean's expression in that moment, the awe and the pleasure, the hope that looked so boyish and dear on his handsome face, and—oh, yeah… lookee there—the lust. They would have to take advantage of that soon. Very, very soon. She had only one more point to make….

"I don't want a fairy tale, anymore, Dean. Really. Well…I wouldn't mind the singing mice…but trying to live in a fairy tale is exhausting. What I need is a man I love and respect, who loves and respects me. I expect our marriage to be the shelter and strength for our family. So I'm not going to run away anymore. This is my life, and I intend to stand and fight for it."

She put both fists on her hips. "Now. You're coming home with me, Dean Kingsley. And don't get lippy about it. You give me any guff, and you'll see what angry does to a librarian."

His eyes glowed a deep spring-blue she wouldn't mind looking at every day for the rest of her life. Stepping around the table, Dean stood close enough to swap pheromones and sent his gaze appreciatively up and down his very adamant wife. "I love it when you go gangsta."

Taking her face in his hands, he kissed her, that honey-pouring, knee-melting, I-know-you-and-love-you kiss that she'd like to bottle for use every day when they were apart for more than, say, ten minutes. This was what she had almost given up.

When he lifted his head, he remembered they had an audience of one. Keeping a hand on Rosemary's back (and making sensuously slow circles that could drive a girl crazy), Dean addressed the woman who, at the moment, looked as if she'd been in a bad episode of *Punked*. "Esmeralda, this is my wife, Rosemary. Rosie, this is Dr. Esmeralda Duran. She'll be working with Dr. Gill until Clinica Adelina is up and running. Then she'll head the health center."

"Oh, hello! A pleasure to meet you." Rosemary leaned forward to offer her hand, which Dr. Duran took warily.

"Uh-huh. Why don't I leave you two alone...." Esmeralda edged to the alley-entrance door. "Sounds as if you need some time. Dean, thanks so much for showing me the apartment. I'd like to move in a couple of days from now if that's all right." Her coal-black eyes shifted to Rosemary, who understood her hesitation immediately.

"Here's the extra key." She offered it to the other woman. "And no copies have been made. Promise." She was definitely going to have to make a second first impression on Dr. Duran.

Esmeralda plucked the key gingerly from Rosemary's fingers. "Okay, thanks. Well." She nodded again, halfway out the door. "Have a really...interesting evening."

"We will." Rosemary waved. "'Bye." When the door shut behind the beautiful physician, Rosemary cocked her head. "Is she an ob-gyn, by any chance? I could use someone local."

"Hmm," Dean studied his bride. "We may have to shop around."

"Okay." She smiled up at him. "So you're renting your apartment."

"I thought I would, yes. I had hoped to live with my wife till death we did part and all that. But then she realized what a lame-brained jackass I'd been—"

"You weren't that big a jackass—"

"Yes, I was."

He looked sincere and contrite, and she realized this was another apology for the will and that he had to get it off his chest, even though she was ready to move on. "Okay, have it your way."

"Thank you. So I was going to stay away for a couple of days while I figured out how to make a very dramatic statement about how much I love you."

"Really." She smiled brightly. *He said it!* "And what did you come up with?"

Dean raised a brow, wry with regret. "Nothing like what you came up with. I'm going to have to go back to the drawing board."

"Please don't."

Dean shoved his hands in his pockets, a huge disappointment when Rosemary wanted them around her. "You can't get to know someone who's deceiving you. So obviously I have a lot of work ahead, introducing myself to my wife. Becoming the best friend she wants and deserves."

A thrill shot through Rosemary, from her skin all the way down to her soul.

"That sounds time-consuming," she said.

"Bound to be." He nodded solemnly. "Labor-intensive, too. Is your schedule clear?"

"You bet." She nodded back, just as solemnly, picturing weekends at the coast…staying up all night to make love…a hundred second honeymoons…. Heaven. "Of course, five months from now your daughter will have something to say about our free time."

"Daughter." Dean's solemn expression softened to the boyish, wonder-filled sweetness she knew reflected the best of his heart. "A girl?"

Rosemary feared her face might not be big enough to host the smile that stretched across it. But her throat tightened when she saw the telltale sparkle fill her husband's eyes.

"With her mother's curls," he said, reaching out—finally!—to gather Rosemary into his arms.

"And your eyes, I hope." She snuggled against him. "I think I'll teach her to talk gangsta."

Dean's chest bounced beneath her ear. "Librarian gangsta."

Rosemary socked him lightly. They kissed until it was time to come up for air then she leaned back and said, "Want to begin getting to know each other *really* well?"

Brushing the curls off her forehead, Dean nodded, a man who knew exactly what he wanted and understood that he already had it. "We've got at least fifty years of intense work ahead of us. May as well get started."

"May as well."

Rosemary grinned. Once upon a time, she'd chased a fairy tale. Now she stood squarely in the middle of reality and it was everything she'd ever dreamed. Plus a whole lot more.

* * * * *

Look for the next book in
HOME SWEET HONEYFORD,
coming in 2011,
wherever Harlequin Books are sold.

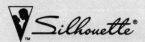

SPECIAL EDITION

COMING NEXT MONTH

Available March 29, 2011

REQUEST YOUR FREE BOOKS!

2 FREE NOVELS PLUS 2 FREE GIFTS!

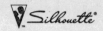

SPECIAL EDITION
Life, Love and Family!

YES! Please send me 2 FREE Silhouette Special Edition® novels and my 2 FREE gifts (gifts are worth about $10). After receiving them, if I don't wish to receive any more books, I can return the shipping statement marked "cancel." If I don't cancel, I will receive 6 brand-new novels every month and be billed just $4.24 per book in the U.S. or $4.99 per book in Canada. That's a saving of at least 15% off the cover price! It's quite a bargain! Shipping and handling is just 50¢ per book in the U.S. and 75¢ per book in Canada.* I understand that accepting the 2 free books and gifts places me under no obligation to buy anything. I can always return a shipment and cancel at any time. Even if I never buy another book, the two free books and gifts are mine to keep forever.

235/335 SDN FC7H

Name	(PLEASE PRINT)

Address	Apt. #

City	State/Prov.	Zip/Postal Code

Signature (if under 18, a parent or guardian must sign)

Mail to the Reader Service:
IN U.S.A.: P.O. Box 1867, Buffalo, NY 14240-1867
IN CANADA: P.O. Box 609, Fort Erie, Ontario L2A 5X3

Not valid for current subscribers to Silhouette Special Edition books.

Want to try two free books from another line?
Call 1-800-873-8635 or visit www.ReaderService.com.

* Terms and prices subject to change without notice. Prices do not include applicable taxes. Sales tax applicable in N.Y. Canadian residents will be charged applicable taxes. Offer not valid in Quebec. This offer is limited to one order per household. All orders subject to credit approval. Credit or debit balances in a customer's account(s) may be offset by any other outstanding balance owed by or to the customer. Please allow 4 to 6 weeks for delivery. Offer available while quantities last.

Your Privacy—The Reader Service is committed to protecting your privacy. Our Privacy Policy is available online at www.ReaderService.com or upon request from the Reader Service.

We make a portion of our mailing list available to reputable third parties that offer products we believe may interest you. If you prefer that we not exchange your name with third parties, or if you wish to clarify or modify your communication preferences, please visit us at www.ReaderService.com/consumerschoice or write to us at Reader Service Preference Service, P.O. Box 9062, Buffalo, NY 14269. Include your complete name and address.

SSE11

Selene wanted nothing to do with the father of her son, Alex; but Aristedes had other plans…that included them.

Read on for an sneak peek from
THE SARANTOS SECRET BABY *by Olivia Gates, available April 2011, only from Harlequin Desire.*

"You were right to turn my marriage offer down," Aristedes said.

And Selene found her voice at last, found the words that would not betray the blow he'd dealt her. "Thanks for letting me know. You didn't have to come all the way here, though. You could have just let it go. I left yesterday with the understanding that this case is closed."

Before the hot needles behind her eyes could dissolve into an unforgivable display of stupidity and weakness, she began to close the door.

The door stopped against an immovable object. His flat palm.

"I can't accept that." His voice was low, leashed.

What did her tormentor mean now? Was he ending one game only to start another?

She raised eyes as bruised as her self-respect to his, found nothing there but solemnity and determination.

Before she could voice her confusion, he elaborated. "I never let anything go unless I'm certain it's unworkable. I realize I made you an unworkable offer, and that's why I'm withdrawing it. I'm here to offer something else. A workability study."

She leaned against the door, thankful for its support and partial shield. "Your son and I are not a business venture you can test for feasibility."

His gaze grew deeper, made her feel as if he was trying to delve into her mind, take control of it. "It's actually the other way around. I'm the one who would be tested."

She shook her head. "Why bother? I know—and *you* know—you're not workable. Not with me."

His spectacular eyebrows lowered over eyes she felt were emitting silver hypnosis. "You're right again. Neither you nor I have any reason to believe that isn't the truth. The only truth. It might be best for both you and Alex to never hear from me again, to forget I exist. But then again, maybe not. I'm only asking for the chance for both of us to find out for certain. You believe I'm unworkable in any personal relationship. I've lived my life based on that belief about myself. I never really had reason to question it. But I have one now. In fact, I have two."

Find out what happens in
THE SARANTOS SECRET BABY by Olivia Gates,
available April 2011, only from Harlequin Desire.

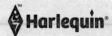